Dead Messages

KRISTEN BRAND

This is a work of fiction. Names, characters, places, and incidents either are the product of the author's imagination or are used fictitiously. Any resemblance to actual persons, living or dead, events, or locales is entirely coincidental.

Proofreading services by Victory Editing

Cover design by Kristen Brand

Cover stock images via Pixabay

Published by Kristen Brand

Contents

Acknowledgements

I owe a huge thank you to many people for helping this book come to life.

First, to my beta readers, Mom and J.E., for looking over the manuscript and giving me feedback.

Next, to Annie for her eagle-eyed proofreading.

To all you readers out there for supporting me and helping spread the word about my books.

And to Ron for everything.

Chapter 1

People are trash, especially Glenda

Sydney was cooking dinner when her phone dinged. Turning down the heat on the stove top so her tomato sauce wouldn't splatter everywhere, she picked up her phone and glanced at the new message.

Glenda
I need you to come in tomorrow at 7.

Oh heck no. Sydney's muscles clenched tighter than when she'd gotten her first body piercing, and her thumbs darted across the screen as she typed a reply.

Sydney
Tomorrow's my day off, remember?
I requested it a month ago. You approved it.

Glenda
Change of plans. Last-minute wedding order.
I need you to come in.

Sydney
Have you checked with Marissa or Javier?

Glenda
They're already coming. All hands on deck.

Sydney
I can't make it. It's my sister's birthday.

We're going camping. We have reservations.

Glenda fired off texts like she was shooting bullets and Sydney was a zombie she wanted to ensure never rose again.

Glenda

If you're not willing to pitch in and help, then maybe you shouldn't work here anymore.

This is a huge order, and I need everyone to do their part.

I don't think you realize how much work it takes to keep this bakery in business, and I can't do it without support.

We're a team at Summertime Sweets. If you're not a team player, then I don't see you having a future with us.

Sydney leaned back against the kitchen counter and groaned. She wasn't a slacker. She worked her butt off in the bakery, so shouldn't she be entitled to use her vacation days? One of these days, she'd give Glenda a piece of her mind—when she had another job lined up, which wasn't today.

Sydney
Fine.
See you tomorrow.

Sydney paced up and down her apartment. Long and narrow, it was a good space for pacing. The rooms lined up one after the other: bedroom, bathroom, kitchen, and living/dining room. It ended with a balcony she could only use five months out of the year because Michigan was a barren winter wasteland. Boring cream-colored paint covered the walls, the carpet an even duller brown. She'd done her best to personalize the place, mostly with framed concert posters and potted plants that gave her something green to look at in the aforementioned barren winter wasteland.

She should've just told Glenda no. Sydney had been told

she was intimidating—mostly by people who didn't like her tattoos and blue-dyed hair. Five feet seven and pale from lack of sun, she didn't feel intimidating, but she wished she could channel some of that menace and get Glenda to back off.

Sighing, she texted her sister.

Sydney

I'm so sorry. I'm going to be late tomorrow. We can't carpool. You'll have to drive up on your own.

Alex

Oh no! Everything okay?

Sydney

Fine. The Frosting Führer is ordering me to go in. I freaking knew this was going to happen.

Alex

Didn't you request it off?

Sydney

YES. A month ago.

Alex

I'm sorry. 🙁

Sydney felt a fond warmth in her chest, looking at the message. Her sister had a bad habit of apologizing for things that weren't her fault. She was pretty much the sweetest person ever; sometimes it made Sydney doubt they were related.

Sydney

Don't apologize. I'm the one who's screwing up your birthday party.

Alex
You're not screwing it up. You can still come, right?

Sydney
Yeah, I'll drive up as soon as I get off.

Alex
Cool.
I just feel bad. You don't seem like you've been happy at work lately.

Was it that obvious? Sydney's pacing took her to the living room, and she flopped down on the couch.

Sydney
I like what I do. Nowhere else around here is going to pay me to make galaxy unicorn cupcakes or a cake that looks like a human brain.
It's just the hours suck and Glenda's a demanding control freak.
I dunno. Maybe I should ask Caleb about that restaurant he went to work at after he quit last week.

Alex
NO.
Don't talk to Caleb. I thought you two broke up?

Sydney
We did. That doesn't mean we can't talk.

Alex
When you talk, it ends with you hooking up.
He's trash.

Sydney
All men are trash.

Alex
Not true.

Sydney
You're right. Let me fix that:
People in general are trash.

Three dots appeared on the screen as Alex typed, and Sydney waited. Was her sister composing an essay for her reply?

Alex
There are nice people out there. You just don't meet them because you're spending all your time with the walking dumpster fire that is Caleb. And if you want to give me the best birthday present ever, delete his number.
Seriously, don't text him.

Sydney had already closed the conversation with Alex and was scrolling through her messages to find Caleb's name. Her sister's next text popped up at the top of the screen.

Alex
You're texting him now, aren't you?

Sydney had no good way to answer that, so she took the coward's way out and didn't reply.

• • •

Sydney
Hey.

Caleb
Hey, sexy.

Sydney
How's the new job?

Caleb
Not bad. The manager's cool. She leaves me alone unless I need help.

Sydney
I'm so jealous.

Caleb
I know, right?

Sydney
So what have you been baking?

Caleb
Nothing lately. I need to go grocery shopping.
Why? You want to come over for dinner?

He sent a GIF of a romantic-looking dinner, the table topped with candles and a vase of red roses. Sydney rolled her eyes. He'd never put that much effort into a dinner when they'd been together, and they'd dated on and off for two years, so he'd had plenty of opportunity.

She needed to make sure their breakup stuck this time. Alex was right. Whenever they talked, Sydney ended up hooking up with him no matter how hard she swore not to. And since they had worked in the same bakery, he'd been impossible to avoid. They would chat about something innocuous like the birthday cake they were baking, and he'd tell a funny story about how his last birthday had ended with him doing karaoke in a Spider-Man costume. Sydney would laugh, and before she knew it, they'd be going out for drinks after their shift.

On second thought, getting a job in the same restaurant as him was about as intelligent as an alcoholic starting work in a brewery. What if she fell back into old habits? Assuming she got hired, she'd have to keep busy and avoid talking to him. She could even schedule her shifts for when he wasn't working as much as possible. But would that be enough, or was she setting herself up for another two years of bad breakups and even worse reconciliations?

It was his stupid face's fault. She'd be able to resist him if he weren't so good-looking—and charming. That charm was the reason it had taken her almost two months to realize he was a lazy, insensitive flake.

Sydney
No. I mean at the restaurant. What type of desserts do they have you making?

Caleb
Nothing. I just prep lunch and dinner—chopping vegetables and meat and stuff.

Sydney
I thought you applied for a pastry chef position?

Caleb
No openings.

Sydney
Dang it.

Caleb
Hoping I could score you a new job away from Glenda?

Sydney
Yeah.

Caleb
What'd she do now?

Sydney sucked in a noisy breath through her nose. She had to loosen her grip on the phone before she could reply, her hands clenched tight like she was trying to crush it. She should really buy a stress ball or something. All this pent-up aggression couldn't be good for her.

Sydney
Alex's birthday is tomorrow. She's been planning a big camping trip for months.
I got approval to take the day off, but Glenda just told me to come in tomorrow or get fired.

Caleb
That sucks, sorry.
Want me to see if I can get you a job here anyway? You'd be a good waitress.

Sydney
Seriously? I'd be a terrible waitress. Too antisocial.

Caleb
Yeah, but you're hot. Guys would leave you big tips.

He really didn't know her at all, did he? And they'd dated for two years.

Sydney
Look, thanks for the offer, but I want a job that involves baking.
Guess that means I'm stuck with Glenda for now.

Caleb
Want me to cheer you up? I could come over.

Sydney
No, thanks. I gotta go in early tomorrow. Anyway, we're done, remember?

Caleb
You can't blame a guy for trying.

Sydney
I'm going to sleep. Talk to you later.

Caleb
Later.

And hey, don't let Glenda get you down. She's a jerk to everyone, and people like that always get what they deserve.

Chapter 2

Nobody gets paid enough for this

Sydney woke bright and early the next morning and made a mental note to send Alex a happy birthday text later. (Waking her up with a text message at six in the morning would *not* be a thoughtful birthday present.) She threw her overnight bag in the trunk of the car and carefully—so carefully—put Alex's birthday cake in the back seat.

Sydney had finished baking it the day before. It looked minimalist and modern: round with smooth white buttercream frosting and no decoration. But Sydney had separated the batter into six bowls and added food coloring before recombining them and baking. Once Alex cut into the cake, it would reveal a bright rainbow swirl. If Alex didn't freak out and squeal, Sydney would swear off black and wear pastels for the rest of her life.

She drove extra slowly, every pothole in Beaverfield's battered roads a potential cake-wrecking disaster. It was late April, and the last snowfall had melted a week earlier, so at least she didn't have to worry about slick roads. Still, she breathed a sigh of relief when she pulled into the parking lot with the cake intact.

Summertime Sweets sat in a nice little strip mall. A tutoring center occupied the space on the left of it, attracting plenty of kids who begged their parents to buy them a cookie or cupcake. Sydney sometimes treated herself at the nail salon a few spots down and grabbed takeout from the tiny pizza place when she felt too tired to cook. The only eyesore had been the vacant storefront to the right of the bakery, the awful diner that used to exist there having finally gone out of business the year before. (Sydney had eaten there precisely once and still shuddered at the memory of the sticky, unwashed table and lukewarm food.)

Construction had been going on there for the past week, and she hoped a decent restaurant moved in this time. Beaverfield had depressingly few good places to eat at.

The sound of drills and hammers drifted out from within the building as Sydney walked toward the bakery. But the noise didn't drown out the sound of Glenda, who was arguing with a man on the sidewalk.

"It's too much noise!" she shouted. "How do you expect us to get any work done over here?"

"Look, I know it's loud," said the man. "But what do you want from me? We're doing construction."

He must be the new tenant. A tall, lean Asian man, he looked to be around her age: thirty or so. He had a stylish haircut, longer on top with strands sweeping across his forehead and shorter on the back and sides. The stubble on his face wasn't quite thick enough to call a beard, but it was definitely more deliberate than a five-o'clock shadow. Wearing dark jeans and a gray jacket, he skirted the edge between a casual and professional look.

"You need to be more considerate of your neighbors," Glenda said. "The machinery is practically rattling the windows! How can we bake with all this racket? And the customers!" She clutched her chest like loud noises killed more people than heart disease. "They're looking for a cozy, welcoming atmosphere—not jackhammers attacking their eardrums."

"Again, I'm sorry for the inconvenience." The man kept his tone calm, though his furrowed brow revealed she was getting to him. "We should be done by the end of next week."

"A whole week?" Glenda shrieked. "That's completely unacceptable."

"I don't know what to tell you. We can't remodel the place with masking tape and prayers. There's going to be noise."

"Do the work when we're closed."

He gave her a flat stare. "You're open seven days a week."

She crossed her arms and glared back at him. "In the evenings after we're gone."

"That's ridiculous." He ran a hand through his hair. "The contractors can't work on that schedule. You'll just have to put up with it for a week."

"I'll be talking to the landlord about this!"

He snapped his fingers. "That's the first good idea I've heard from you. Please. Go bother him instead of me."

He stormed into the restaurant, leaving Glenda gaping. Sydney mentally applauded him for getting through the conversation without any profanity.

"Sydney!"

Glenda's voice made her jump.

Her boss's eyes narrowed suspiciously. "What's that you're holding?"

"My sister's birthday cake," Sydney said. "It'll go bad in the car, so I'm putting it in the fridge."

"The fridge isn't for personal use."

Sydney's hands tightened around the Tupperware. She fought to follow the new tenant's example and keep her voice calm. "I'm already going to be late to the party because you asked me to come in last minute. If I have to go home to pick up the cake, I'll be even later. The fridge has plenty of room. I don't see the problem."

Glenda's nostrils flared. If she refused… What was Sydney supposed to do—dump the cake on the sidewalk?

"Fine," Glenda said. "Stop dawdling out here and start making buttercream. We have two hundred cupcakes to frost."

And she stomped into the bakery, leaving Sydney standing outside with a cake and an extremely bad mood.

• • •

Summertime Sweets had a bright, cheerful interior. Customers probably never guessed how miserable all the employees felt working there. With a white tile floor and pale pink walls, it aimed for a summery feel. Framed vintage illustrations showed people at the seaside, and porcelain plates on display shelves bore images of pink flamingos and tropical plants. A few tables and chairs inside offered customers a place to eat, and a long glass case along the counter showed off the good stuff: cupcakes, cookies, pastries, pies, and donuts to name a few.

Sydney bypassed it all and headed to the kitchen in the back, waving at her coworker Marissa. She put Alex's cake in the industrial fridge (It was barely half-full, so what was Glenda's problem?) and grabbed some sticks of butter so they would start to soften.

Marissa glanced over her shoulder to check that Glenda was in her office. "I can't believe she made you come in today."

"I can," Sydney grumbled, setting up a stand mixer.

"How many hours have you put in this week already? She doesn't pay us enough for this."

"I don't think there's enough money in the world to properly compensate someone for putting up with Glenda Whitaker."

Marissa snickered as she rolled out cookie dough.

She and Sydney had gone to the same high school, though Marissa had been two years ahead of her. She had a round face and fair skin, her hair long with thick bangs and dyed a shade of auburn that pushed the limit of natural. She wore jeans and a teal sweater, and her apron had a cute floral pattern.

Sydney pulled on her own apron, which was black and had a grinning skull on the front. "Speaking of which, did you ask her for a raise yet?"

Marissa put more force behind the rolling pin. "No."

"You better woman up and do it soon."

"I know, I know. It's just…" She sighed. "I'm afraid

she's going to say no."

"She's almost definitely going to say no."

Marissa slammed down a cookie cutter with the force of an axe. "Wow. Thanks for the encouragement."

"What can I say? I'm a pessimist. But at least you'll know for sure that way. You can start job hunting or adjust your budget or whatever you need to do."

Marissa groaned. "Don't make me think about my budget. If I'm wearing a paper bag on Monday, it's because I sold my entire wardrobe to pay rent."

Sydney paused midway through measuring powdered sugar. "If you need anything—"

"It's fine. I'll figure it out. I should finish up here and get started on the chocolate ganache."

Sydney looked around. "Where's Javier? I thought he was coming in today."

"He was, but his car broke down. He's stuck at the mechanic's."

Sydney thought of a boring waiting room and expensive repair bill. "Some guys have all the luck."

Conversation died off as they focused on work. The last-minute wedding order on top of all their usual baking had the two of them rushing around. Thirty minutes passed in a blur, and then the door to Glenda's office swung open and she burst out like an angry lion from a cage. Faith, her daughter and the assistant manager, hurried after her.

The two women looked a lot alike. They had the same rectangular faces and pear-shaped bodies, and their eyes were the same shade of blue. They both wore glasses, though Glenda's were larger. Glenda was pushing seventy, her chin-length hair curly and gray and her wrinkles deepened by years of scowling. Faith was in her midforties, her fine blond hair short and layered. One might say she looked exactly like Glenda had twenty years earlier, but Glenda had probably never worn the anxious expression that constantly graced Faith's face.

"But if we just spent a little more on advertising—"

Faith started.

"Don't you think we threw enough money down the drain on that already?" Glenda snapped.

Faith nervously smoothed down her apron. "We didn't know what we were doing then. I've been taking some courses online and—"

"I said no."

"We don't have to drop a fortune. We can start—"

Glenda stopped walking and rounded on her. "I don't want to hear it. Grab some cupcake liners and get started on the ones Sydney's finished. You can handle something that simple without screwing it up, right?"

Glenda stalked over to the ovens, leaving Faith with her shoulders slumped. Sydney and Marissa shared a glance and got back to work.

• • •

Two hundred cupcakes, three sheet cakes, and one three-tier wedding cake later, Sydney trudged out the back door. The air was frigid despite the afternoon sun, and she hadn't put on her jacket, not planning to stay outside for long. Hauling a massive garbage bag in each hand, she headed to the dumpster. The new tenant from next door was already there, tossing a bag of construction debris inside.

"Hey," Sydney said. "Can you—"

"No, I can't make the machinery quieter or buy you noise-canceling headphones or only do construction on Tuesdays when the moon is full," he said, striding toward the restaurant without even looking at her.

"Funny." She held up the garbage bags. "I was going to ask if you could hold the dumpster open. My hands are full."

He stared at her for a moment. Then, stiffly, he walked back over and held it open so she could throw in the bags.

"Thanks," she said.

"No problem." His gaze dropped to the pavement.

"And uh… Sorry about that."

"No worries. You've got PGS."

His eyebrows shot up. "Excuse me?"

"PGS. Post Glenda Syndrome. Stress caused from interacting with my boss. Symptoms include irritability, jitters, and tears, and the only treatment I've found is swiping cookies from the display case when she's not looking."

His mouth curved upward, and dang—that was an attractive smile.

"Good to know," he said. "And I'll take that cookie if you're offering."

"I'll see what I can do." She held out her hand. "I'm Sydney Farina."

"Logan Kobayashi."

He shook her hand. His grip was firm and his hand callused, and he smelled nice and masculine, a mix of citrusy cologne and a hint of sawdust from the construction.

"I'm glad your restaurant is opening," she said. "This entire town has maybe three good places to eat, so don't let Glenda scare you off."

"I've been working toward this for ten years. It'll take more than a pushy geriatric to stop me."

"Good attitude." She gestured at the door behind her. "Well, I'd better get back in there."

"What time do you get off?" he asked.

"I should be done by four. I'll swing by with the cookie on my way out."

His voice took on a low, tantalizing timbre. "I wasn't asking because of the cookie."

Oh.

Sydney met his gaze and felt heat rise in her body despite the cold air. She couldn't remember the last time someone had asked her out—someone who wasn't Caleb anyway.

"Do you have plans for tonight?" Logan asked.

"Yeah, actually. It's my sister's birthday."

"Another time then?"

Sydney considered it—but not for very long.

"How about I give you my number, and we can go from there?"

• • •

At four o'clock, Sydney hung up her apron and pulled on her jacket. Faith was wiping down the tables. (Sydney had already cleaned them, but Faith was a neat freak, so Sydney didn't take it personally.) Marissa checked that all the ovens were turned off, and Glenda took out the cash register drawer to balance the day's transactions.

Sydney pulled Alex's cake from the fridge. "I'm out," she said. "Later, everyone."

Faith looked up from the tables. "Have a good night."

"Have fun camping!" Marissa called from the back. "Try not to get eaten by a bear."

"I'll see you tomorrow at noon," Glenda said. "And Sydney?"

Glenda hesitated, her mouth twisting like she'd just bitten into a cake where the baker had used salt instead of sugar.

"Thank you for coming in today," she said finally.

Sydney looked away. "Yeah, sure. See you tomorrow."

Chapter 3

Life sucks, then you die

That evening, Sydney sat by a campfire and ate her second s'more. The temperature had plummeted, and she was bundled up in a scarf, knit cap, and gloves with a design of skeleton hands. Evergreen trees surrounded the campsite, the clear sky giving an excellent view of the stars overhead. Sydney could hear owls hooting and water lapping gently against the lakeshore—in her imagination anyway. In reality, the pop music, laughter, and talking drowned out everything else.

Alex was five years younger than Sydney. Tall and thin, she had big brown eyes and dirty-blond hair cropped only a few inches long in a stylish, shaggy look. She was currently standing on a log and singing along off-key to the music as her friends cheered her on. (Calling it *singing* was generous; it was more like boisterous shouting.) Sydney was chilling with a beer, having outgrown her wild partier phase years ago. Still, she had a pleasant buzz and was happy to sit back and let the atmosphere wash over her. Alex was having fun, and that was all that mattered.

Sydney's phone buzzed in her pocket, and she winced. That had better not be Glenda…

Logan
Hey. Hope you're having a good time at your sister's party.

She blamed the heat that rose in her cheeks on the beer. It was nice of him to text. She snapped a photo of the campfire and sent it back to him.

Sydney
Thanks. So far, so good.

Logan
I didn't realize you were camping.

Sydney
Yeah, I thought I was going to hate it, but it's not so bad. And my sister's friends want to tell ghost stories later, so I'm looking forward to scaring the crap out of them.

Logan
You've got an evil side, huh?

Sydney
You bet.
So what are you doing tonight?

Logan
Leaving the restaurant now. I'll probably just crash when I get home.

Sydney
You're just now leaving?!

Logan
There's a lot of work to do.

Sydney
Wow.
You'd better pour yourself a beer or something when you get home.

Logan
Oh, I plan to.

"Yes!" Alex shouted, making Sydney look up. "Brilliant idea!"

Alex jumped down from the log, stumbled, and nearly face-planted. Wobbly but enthusiastic, she raised a fist into the air and called out like a general marshaling an army. "To the canoes!"

"The canoes!" everyone shouted, standing up and following her toward the lake.

Sydney groaned.

Sydney
Crap. Got to go.
My sister is super drunk and just decided canoeing is a good idea.
I need to go stop her from drowning.

Logan
Good luck.

Sydney
Thanks.
If you're back at the restaurant tomorrow, my shift starts at noon.
If not, see you on Monday.

Sydney managed to divert everyone from the canoes by distracting them with cake, and the night ended with nothing worse happening than a few bruises and some vomit. Despite the cold temperatures and hard ground beneath the tent, she slept like a log.

The next morning, she woke up before everyone else and drove fifteen minutes down the road to the grocery store. By the time Alex crawled out of her tent, blinking and groaning, Sydney had used the grill to make breakfast tacos with eggs, peppers, and onions. She handed Alex a plastic cup of water and two aspirin first.

"You," Alex said, "are my favorite sister."

"Don't let Savannah hear you say that."

"I don't care." Alex gave her a crushing hug. "You're the best."

Everyone gradually staggered out of the tents over the next hour, gushing over Sydney's breakfast. Sydney stayed long enough to clean up and make sure Alex felt well enough to drive. Then she hit the road. Saturday-morning traffic wasn't bad, and she pulled into the bakery's parking lot at ten before noon.

Flashing sirens greeted her.

Sydney's stomach flipped. Police cars and ambulances filled the parking lot. Had something happened at the bakery? At Logan's restaurant? Were the kids at the tutoring center okay? She slowed down and tried to see what was going on, but the first responders were spread out in front of all three storefronts. She couldn't tell which business had the emergency.

Sydney's hands shook as she parked and pulled the keys from the ignition. Maybe it was nothing—a false alarm. Or maybe the local teens had spray-painted graffiti on the back of the building again, and Glenda had overreacted and called the cops. That didn't explain the ambulance though. Had one of the construction workers had an accident?

Sydney hurried toward the building and saw Faith nodding numbly as a police officer spoke to her.

Faith turned, her eyes red and shiny streaks of tears running down her cheeks. "Sydney!"

She rushed up, hugged Sydney, and wept softly into her shoulder.

"What's wrong?" Sydney stiffened and awkwardly hugged her back. "What happened?"

"It's Mom. When I got here this morning, she was lying on the floor. She— She's—"

Faith shuddered and sobbed again.

Sydney felt like someone had shoved ice down her throat. Glenda was dead? She'd seemed fine yesterday. She'd been baking cakes and shouting orders—just her normal grouchy self.

Every bad thing Sydney had ever thought about her boss cycled through her head, and she felt vaguely sick with guilt.

"Oh, Faith. I'm so sorry."

Faith rubbed her eyes, and the police seemed content to let her cry it out with Sydney for now. Sydney saw more of them inside the bakery through the windows. Was Glenda's corpse just out of sight? Had they put her in a body bag yet, or was she just lying there, eyes open and staring? Sydney shivered.

"Do they know what happened?" Sydney asked. "Did she fall? Was it a heart attack or something like that?"

Faith wiped her nose and shook her head. "I saw her, Sydney. It was awful. Her head's completely bashed in. There's blood everywhere."

The air in Sydney's lungs froze, and she couldn't seem to inhale. She knew what that meant even before Faith said the words.

"Someone killed her."

Chapter 4

Proof things can always get worse

An hour and a half later, Sydney was still sitting outside the bakery. The police had just finished questioning her, but she didn't want to leave Faith alone yet. Apparently her wife had run into trouble finding someone to watch their kids but was on her way now.

The sky was appropriately gray and gloomy, and it felt colder than it had last night even though the temperature must have been at least ten degrees higher. Sydney sat at a bright white table with a cheery yellow umbrella meant for customers to use for eating cupcakes in nice weather; it didn't feel like it belonged at a murder scene. People going to and from the other businesses in the strip mall stared curiously, and reporters had shown up. Sydney avoided everyone's gazes.

She pulled out her phone, looking for a distraction, and saw a barrage of text messages she'd missed while it was on silent mode.

12:54
Javier
My brother-in-law just said there was a murder at the bakery?? Do you know what's going on?

1:12
Marissa
I just heard what happened. Were you there?

1:24
Alex
Where are you? I heard something happened at the bakery. Text me when you get this please.

1:31
Alex
Sydney, are you okay?
Please text me back.

1:32
Alex
Sydney?

Shoot. How had Alex found out so fast? Probably from one of the reporters. Alex was a freelance writer and sometimes did articles for the local paper.

Sydney
I'm okay.

Her sister's response was instantaneous.

Alex
Thank goodness.
What's going on?

Sydney
Glenda's dead.
Can I call you later?

Alex
Oh my gosh.
And yes. Talk to you soon.

"Soon" turned out to be after three o'clock. Sydney trudged up the steps to her apartment and locked the door behind her once she got inside. She did the chain lock in addition to the regular one, feeling paranoid. Or was it really paranoia when someone had literally been murdered in your workplace?

She still couldn't believe it. Glenda was dead. Someone had *killed* her.

Sydney took a shower, feeling unclean in a way that soap and water didn't really fix. Then she poured herself a glass of wine, a sweet white from a local cellar. Settling on the couch, she wrapped herself in her favorite blanket (soft and black with a pattern of cute little vampire bats) and called Alex.

"Hey. I can talk now."

"Where are you?" Alex demanded.

"Home. I needed a shower and a drink."

Alex let out a noisy breath into the speaker, and her voice lost some of its tension. "I can imagine. Is Glenda really dead?"

"Yeah. Looks like it happened sometime last night. She never made it home."

"That's awful. Poor Faith. I'll have to send her flowers."

Sydney thought back to the times Alex had stopped by the bakery. Had she ever seen the two of them interact?

"I didn't realize you two knew each other well."

Alex snorted. "Do you have any idea how small the gay community in this town is? I know everyone. But what happened to Glenda? Was it a stroke?"

Sydney tried to think of a way to say it without sounding ominous and dramatic but couldn't.

"Murder."

"What?" Alex shrieked.

Sydney winced and pulled the phone a few inches away from her ear. "Yeah. The safe in her office was cleaned out. Looks like she was killed for the money."

"I can't believe it. That's horrible."

Sydney took a gulp of wine. "I haven't gotten to the worst part."

"What could be worse than murder?"

"Faith said the door was unlocked when she went in this morning, and I heard the police saying there was no sign of forced entry." Sydney felt a lump in her throat and swallowed. "So the murderer must have had a key."

"What? No. What if someone just left the door unlocked?"

Sydney leaned back against a throw pillow. "I'm trying to tell myself that, but I know Glenda. She always made sure the building was locked up tight after closing. I think she saw some teenagers loitering outside once and convinced herself they were going to rob her. I used to think she was being paranoid, but…"

"Who has keys?"

"All the full-time employees. So me, Marissa, and Faith. Javier too, now that I think about it. He's part-time, but he opens on Tuesdays and Thursdays."

"You can't think one of them is the killer?"

"I don't know!" Sydney lurched up from the couch, getting tangled in the blanket. She flung it aside and started pacing. "I don't want to suspect any of them, but one of them must have done it. Maybe I can rule out Javier since his car broke down... But he could have taken an Uber or something, so no."

"His car broke down? When?"

"Yesterday morning. He couldn't make it in."

Alex was silent for a moment. "Weird."

Weird? Not a word Sydney wanted to hear at that moment.

"What?" she asked.

"When I was leaving for the campground yesterday, I stopped to get gas," Alex said slowly. "He was there filling up his car."

"You're sure it was him?"

"Yeah, I've seen him at the bakery a few times. And we ran into him and his family at the Renaissance Fair, remember?"

Sydney remembered. But Javier couldn't have killed Glenda.

Well, physically he could have. He was huge, probably six feet five and as broad as a bus. He was also the sweetest, softest teddy bear of a man you could ever meet. He wore ridiculous aprons with cute cartoon cats on them and could always cheer up the kids in the shop when they had a sugar-induced meltdown—which made sense since he had four kids of his own.

And he'd lied about where he was on Friday.

"Okay," Sydney said. "I'm officially freaking out now. Did he see you?"

"I don't think so," Alex said. "And this doesn't mean he's a murderer! People lie to get out of work all the time. Or did you not tell Glenda you had a stomach bug so you could go to that goth rock concert last month?"

"It was death metal."

Alex harrumphed at her. "You know what I mean. I still think Glenda probably just didn't lock the door. It's not dark yet when you close. She probably felt safe enough inside even if she was by herself."

"Maybe." Sydney readjusted her grip on the phone, her hand sore from clutching it so tightly. "The police are going to interview all the employees though."

"You have a key. They don't suspect you, do they?"

"I hope not. I told them about your party. There's like a dozen people who can vouch for me being there all night. Plus I left the bakery before Faith and Marissa."

Not that any of that had stopped her stomach from heaving nauseously as she spoke to the cop who'd interviewed her.

"Good," Alex said. "I still can't believe it. You hear about this stuff on the news but never expect it to happen to someone so close."

"I know."

Sydney's tone must have given away more than she meant to, because Alex's voice turned soft and sympathetic.

"How are you feeling? Do you want me to come over?"

"Not now," Sydney said. "I need some time to myself."

"Okay, but call me if you need anything."

They said goodbye, and as Sydney sat back down on the couch and looked at the clock, she felt weirdly lost. The rest of the day stretched out before her, and she didn't have the first clue what to do with it. Still, at least she *had* a day in which to feel directionless and depressed.

That was more than Glenda could say.

Chapter 5

Nope

Sydney woke at her usual time the next morning, and it took a few seconds for the memories of the day before to hit her—like a semitruck hitting a poor helpless raccoon. She covered her face with her hands, feeling more listless and lethargic than she usually did in the morning. She didn't want to go to work today. Would the bakery even open? Rolling over with a groan, she groped her nightstand clumsily until she found her phone. She needed to text Faith. The screen lit up, nearly blinding her, and she squinted at two text messages she'd received.

12:00 AM
Glenda
Sydney?
Are you there?

5:58 AM
Glenda
Sydney, are you awake?

What the…?

She sat up with a jolt. Her chest seized with pain as her heartbeat went into overdrive. She couldn't be seeing this. Was she still asleep? This wasn't possible.

She rubbed her eyes, but when she looked at her phone again, the messages remained. She wasn't dreaming. She'd gotten two texts from Glenda, and if the time stamps were right, they'd been sent *after* she'd died.

The time stamps must be wrong then. The painful knot

in Sydney's chest started to unwind as she thought it through. Glenda must have texted her days ago but had bad service. That had happened before, Sydney not receiving a random text from Alex or her dad until hours after they'd sent it.

Right. That made sense. Sydney pushed off her blankets and stumbled toward the bathroom. That had been an awful way to start the day, but she'd get over it. Yesterday had started with a murder, so today would have to be better by default.

The phone vibrated in her hand.

Glenda
Answer me.

Sydney's hand shook. She wanted to throw the phone across the room, which was ridiculous. It was just a phone. It couldn't hurt her. She looked around, half expecting to see a camera crew. This *had* to be an elaborate prank, right?

…right?

Okay, first things first. She set down her phone on the bathroom counter and did her business—because otherwise she just might pee her pants in fear. Then she washed her hands and stared at herself in the mirror. She didn't look like a person who'd had a psychotic break overnight and was hallucinating text messages from her dead boss. She just looked tired.

She didn't want to spend all day worrying about whether the messages were a glitch or not. She picked up the phone.

Sydney
Who is this?

She'd expected no response, but three little dots appeared to indicate Glenda was typing. The bathroom spun, and Sydney had to put a hand on the counter to steady herself.

How could Glenda be typing? Her corpse was lying in the morgue.

Glenda
It's Glenda. I need your help.

Sydney
Glenda's dead.
Whoever you are, you're seriously messed up. This isn't funny.

Glenda
I'm not trying to be funny. I was murdered. There's absolutely nothing funny about this situation.

Sydney
Screw you.
Stop texting me, or I'm going to the police.

Glenda
This isn't a joke. I'm trapped in some kind of foggy purgatory, and my phone is only letting me send messages to one person—you.
I don't know what's going on, but you need to help me.
It's your responsibility.

Nope. No way was Sydney falling for whatever the heck this was. Some creep must have gotten ahold of Glenda's phone and decided to play a sick joke. There were some seriously pathetic losers in the world who had way too much free time. Sydney should just treat the texter like an internet troll and ignore them.

She took another shower and then made coffee and oatmeal for breakfast. She was looking through her closet for something to wear when she realized she'd forgotten to text Faith, distracted by the messages from the Glenda impersonator. When she picked up her phone, more waited for her.

6:07
Glenda
Will you reply already? You're acting incredibly immature.

6:12
Glenda
You can't just ignore me.

6:13
Glenda
I have been murdered. Whatever you're doing, it's not more important than what I'm going through.

6:15
Glenda
Stop being selfish. You're the only person who can help me get to the bottom of this.

6:22
Glenda
Please.

Sydney blocked the number. She refused to deal with this sicko on top of everything else. Her phone vibrated a second later, and she nearly swore, but it was just Faith.

Faith
I'm sorry for the late notice, but we're not opening the bakery today. I'll update everyone when I figure out what I'm going to do.

Sydney
If there's anything I can do to help, let me know.

Faith
Thank you.

Sydney got dressed anyway. Lounging around the

apartment in her pajamas all day wasn't going to improve her mental state. She should do something productive with her day off: vacuum the apartment or take her car for an oil change. And she'd been meaning to go through her closet and donate some stuff she never wore anymore. (Who knew? Someone out there might love to get her collection of fishnet stockings.) But she couldn't muster up the energy to do anything.

Her thoughts kept going back to the murder. She might have had better luck keeping her mind off it if that creep hadn't texted her. Who were they anyway? And why had they chosen Sydney to screw around with? Or were they going through Glenda's entire contact list? Sydney hoped not. Faith didn't need that kind of grief.

Goose bumps rose on Sydney's skin. Could the texter be the murderer? Their motive must have been extremely personal if they were going to the trouble of harassing Glenda's acquaintances even after they'd killed her. Who would do something like that?

It couldn't be Javier. It just couldn't.

She sank down on the couch. He'd texted her yesterday after the murder had happened. She should reply. Maybe she could learn something.

Sydney
Sorry I didn't reply to this yesterday. I was kind of overwhelmed.

Javier
Understandable.
How are you holding up?

Sydney
I think I'm still in shock.

Javier
Same.
Glenda was like a force of nature. It's hard to imagine she's gone.

I hope the cops catch whoever did it.

Sydney
Me too.

What now? Sydney couldn't just type "Did you do it?" She didn't think "Where were you yesterday?" would go down so well either. She could ask him if the mechanic had been able to fix his car, but he could easily answer with a lie.

She might mention that Alex saw him at the gas station with a working vehicle, but if Javier *was* the killer, she didn't want to put her sister on his radar—especially not as a witness who could prove he'd lied about his whereabouts on Saturday.

Javier
I'm thinking all us employees could pitch in for a sympathy gift basket for Faith and sign a card. You in?

Sydney
Sure.
Just let me know how much.

Javier
Will do.

Sydney rubbed her head. *There goes the chance to ask him anything useful.* She might as well wave goodbye as it flew out the window.

She could try to bring up the topic in conversation next time she saw him in person… But who was she kidding? Interrogating suspects was the police's job, not hers. She should tell them about his lie if she really thought he was guilty—and she wouldn't do that. He would get hounded by cops when he'd probably just fibbed to get out of work to do something fun.

She leaned her head back against the couch cushion,

wishing the coffee would hurry up and kick in already. Her head felt like it was filled with gelatin. Since she'd replied to Javier's message, she figured that she should text back Marissa too.

Sydney
Hey, sorry for the late reply.

It took about a minute before Marissa responded.

Marissa
No apology necessary.
Can you believe what happened?

Sydney
It doesn't feel real.

Marissa
You weren't the one who found the body, were you?

Sydney
No. Faith got there before me.

Marissa
Oh jeez. I mean, I'm glad it wasn't you, but poor Faith.

Sydney
I know.

Marissa
The cops talked to me yesterday. I'm guessing they interviewed you too?

Sydney
Yeah. I wish I knew if they had any leads.
Did you see anything weird when you left on Saturday?

Marissa

No. I've been racking my brain, but I don't remember anything unusual.

But I left a little after you did. Both Glenda and Faith were still there.

Sydney was about to reply, but then she saw that Marissa was still typing.

Marissa

You don't think Faith had anything to do with it, do you?

Faith? Sydney's gut reaction was to type *no way*, but as she thought about it… Faith had more motive than any of them. Glenda hadn't been able to go a full hour without criticizing her. If a customer canceled an order at the last minute or the bakery ran out of stock of something, you could bet Glenda would blow off steam by snapping at her daughter.

Sydney and the others had dealt with Glenda during the workweek for the past few years, but Faith had been taking her abuse for her entire life. A lot of resentment must have built up over the years.

But Faith had seemed distraught the morning before. Had she been faking it, or had her tears come from guilt and regret?

Sydney

I hope not.

The seconds ticked by as Marissa typed. Was she composing a rock ballad? A murder confession? Whatever she'd typed, she must have changed her mind and deleted it all, because Sydney only got one word.

Marissa

Yeah.

Sydney
This really sucks.

Marissa
You can say that again.
Do you think the bakery will close down? I feel bad, worrying about our jobs when Glenda lost her life, but…

Sydney
I know what you mean.

Sydney had done a bit of online job hunting after talking to Caleb the other night, and it had confirmed that her prospects weren't great. Beaverfield had one other bakery, but it did bread, bagels, and breakfast stuff, not cakes. A few of the restaurants in town served dessert, but their menus were boring.

At Summertime Sweets, Sydney got to make incredible stuff: a hyperrealistic snake cake for a boy's birthday party or cupcakes topped with severed zombie fingers made of fondant for Halloween. Sure, some people just wanted plain old sugar cookies, but the bakery had developed a reputation for wild desserts over the years. And it wasn't just due to Sydney. Javier could make the cutest cake pops shaped like cartoon characters, and Marissa was an expert at gravity-defying topsy-turvy cakes.

Sydney could probably find another bakery like that, but not nearby. She'd either face a long commute every morning or would have to move—and she didn't want that. She might make fun of Beaverfield, but it was her home. Her sister and dad lived here; Sydney didn't want to leave them.

Would Faith close down the bakery? Glenda had been the one to start the business. Frankly, Sydney had never understood why Faith had gone to work for her mother instead of doing the sensible thing and moving as far away from her as possible.

Sydney
I don't know what Faith will do. She probably doesn't either. It's barely been 24 hours.

Before Marissa could reply, another text popped up on the screen.

Glenda
Sydney, I won't let you ignore me.
I demand you answer.

Sydney jerked and nearly fell off the couch. What the heck? She'd blocked that number.

Marissa
You're right. We'll just have to wait.
Text me if you hear anything?

Sydney stared at the words. Her brain was so busy trying to figure out how the impostor was still texting her that it couldn't seem to process the characters on the screen. She blinked and forced herself to focus. Right. She should reply. Conversations with actual friends took precedence over ones with lying creeps.

Her fingers shook, and she kept hitting the wrong letters. Finally she got out a coherent response.

Sydney
I will. You do the same.

Then she opened her conversation with Glenda—or whoever had Glenda's phone. It was the same number as before. She could scroll up and see all their earlier messages. She clicked on Glenda's profile in her contacts and went to block her number—properly this time—but saw that it was already blocked.

What in the world…?

Sydney
I blocked this number. How the heck are you still texting me, you sicko?

Glenda
I'm dead. I don't think the regular rules apply.
And you tried to block me?!
After everything I've done for you, that's how you respond in my time of need?

Sydney
I don't even know you. Stop pretending to be Glenda.
She might have been a jerk, but she doesn't deserve this kind of disrespect.

Glenda
And now you're name-calling. How juvenile.
Are you the one who did this to me? Did you curse me somehow? I always knew you were a witch.

Sydney
Excuse me??

Glenda
You're always dressed in black. You've got blue hair and all those tattoos. And you're so grim about everything.
It figures you're the only one I can communicate with now that I'm dead.

Sydney swallowed. Whoever this was, they knew her. Or at least they knew what she looked like. Were they stalking her? All her social media was private, so they must have seen her in real life. Then again, if they'd known Glenda, they'd probably gone inside the bakery at some point. They must have seen Sydney there.

Sydney
I'm going to block your number again.
Go find something better to do with your time than trolling people.
Make some friends.
Take scuba diving lessons.
Do recreational drugs.
Just stop texting me.

She put her phone on silent mode and left it on the couch, storming into the bedroom to go through her closet. She was going to gather up her old clothes to donate and then get that oil change. She would have a productive day, and that sicko pretending to be Glenda would *not* ruin it for her.

It took about thirty minutes to get everything she didn't want anymore gathered into two big bags. Then she opened her laptop and Googled where to buy pepper spray, adding it to her to-do list for the day. She might fantasize about tracking down whoever was texting her and punching them in the face, but she had no clue how to actually throw a punch. She needed to protect herself in case the creep came after her in person, especially if he or she was the murderer. (And pepper spray would hurt more than a punch anyway.)

She went to grab her phone before driving off, her chest tight with dread at seeing another text.

Logan
I just found out what happened. Are you okay?

Oh shoot. He'd sent it twenty-five minutes earlier and probably thought she was ignoring him—or that she was in the hospital or something.

Sydney
Just shaken up.

Probably should've texted you the news, sorry.

Logan
It's fine.
I'm just glad you're not hurt.

Sydney
Thanks.
I'm still trying to wrap my head around it. Not used to this kind of thing.
Usually the most violence we get in this town is a flock or two of angry geese.

Logan
Crime is everywhere, even in small towns like this.
People just do their best to ignore it until it's staring them in the face.

Sydney
I guess so.

Logan
Sorry. Too dark?

Sydney
Ha. Don't ever apologize for getting dark with me.

Logan
Is there anything I can do for you?
I could drop off some dinner if you're not feeling up to cooking.
I don't even have to come inside if you don't want.

Sydney
That's nice of you, but I'm good.
I'm going to run some errands and then settle in with takeout, beer, and Netflix.

Logan
Good plan.
I guess the bakery will be closed for a while?

Sydney
Yeah. I'll stop by and see you when it's back open.

Logan
Okay, take care.
Text me if you need anything.

Sydney smiled at the screen. Well, at least one nice thing had happened this morning. Her day was just eighty percent awful so far. Maybe seventy-five percent.

She was about to slip her phone into her purse when it vibrated.

Glenda
I've been thinking about how to prove to you that I'm not an impostor.
And I have an idea.
This happened not long after I hired you. It was your time of the month, and your pants got stained. I loaned you my sweater to tie around your waist and hide it.
You asked me not to tell anyone, and I haven't because I keep my word. So unless you told someone, there's no one else who knows.
So that proves who I am.

Glenda
Sydney?

The phone slipped from Sydney's hands, hitting the carpet of her living room with a thump. She scrambled back from it like it was a venomous spider, her heart pounding, and stared.

Chapter 6

Still no

The next morning, Sydney went to the mall. She'd needed to get out of Beaverfield for a while, and Twelve Oaks Mall in nearby Novi was big and bustling, full of potential distractions. She ordered a coffee at Starbucks and snagged one of the chairs in the seating area. For several minutes, she just sipped and watched people walk by, letting the white noise of countless echoing voices wash over her. Then she pulled out her phone.

She'd wanted to do this in public on the theory that her phone was haunted, and if a ghost came out of it and killed her, there would be witnesses. Someone could tell her dad "I'm sorry for your loss. She fought bravely, but there's no escaping a vengeful ghost." And yes, she knew that made zero sense, but having other people around made her feel better.

Swallowing, she typed out a message.

Sydney
I talked to the police yesterday.

The response came immediately.

Glenda
Finally.
Do you have any idea how long I've been waiting for you to reply?
There's absolutely nothing for me to do here. It's just misty emptiness no matter how far I walk.

The ground is too hard to sleep on—not that I've slept since I died anyway.
Don't ignore me like that again.

There was a brief pause.

Glenda
Why did you talk to the police?

Sydney
Because some creep is using Glenda's phone to screw with me.

Glenda
Are you still in denial?
Get your head out of the sand. I need you to use your brains.

If it *was* an impostor, they were doing an ace impression of Glenda. But as Sydney had tossed and turned in her bed last night, her certainty that the texter was an impostor had faded.

Sydney
The cops said they have the phone in their evidence locker.

Glenda
See? I'm telling the truth.

Sydney
They wouldn't let me see it, so they could be lying.
Or you could work at the station and have access to it.

Glenda
Don't be ridiculous. What police officer would do something so unprofessional?

Sydney
You're the one being ridiculous. Cops are people, and people are

horrible.
I'm not ruling it out.
Anyway, they were supremely unhelpful, so I called my cell phone service provider.

Glenda
And?

Sydney
They were even less helpful. Had no idea what I was talking about.

Glenda
Which is obviously because I'm texting you from beyond the grave—like I've been saying all along.

That was pretty much what Sydney had concluded the night before—but conclusions reached at two a.m. on sleepless nights were generally not to be trusted. She needed more evidence.

Sydney
Maybe.
You want to prove it, send me a photo or a video or something.

Glenda
Don't you think I tried that already? The camera's broken.

Sydney
That's convenient.

Glenda
It certainly isn't! Nothing on this phone is working except when I text you.
I tried calling 911. I tried messaging my daughter.
I can't even look at photos of my grandchildren.

Okay, that sounded horrible. If it really *was* Glenda, and she was telling the truth… Sydney set down the phone and massaged her head as she looked around. A toddler made a mad dash away from his mother and shrieked when she grabbed his hand. Two older women in tracksuits chatted as they power walked in loops around the building. A middle-aged man sat slumped in a chair a few feet away from Sydney, looking like he'd been dragged out on a shopping spree and would cut off his right arm to go home. It all looked so normal. Could Sydney really be texting a dead woman in the midst of it?

Sydney
Then here's what we're going to do.
I'll ask you questions to prove your identity.
Answer right, and maybe I'll believe you're who you say you are.

Glenda
I already told you something only I would know!

Sydney
I'm not convinced yet. Humor me.

Seconds ticked by.

Glenda
Fine.

Right. Game time. Sydney had brainstormed a slew of questions overnight but had narrowed them down to three.

Sydney
Why do we have to sign in when using the employee restroom?

Glenda
Because someone was stealing toilet paper. Rolls would disappear days after I bought them. It was probably Caleb though I could never

prove it.

Sydney
Okay.
Javier wanted to do a Secret Santa last year. What was your response?

Glenda
I told him—quite fairly—that Christmas is one of the busiest times of the year for us and we can't afford to be distracted. If you all really wanted to play that silly game so badly, you could have done it outside business hours.

Sydney
What's the rule for using the microwave?

Glenda
Absolutely no personal use. You can bring cold sandwiches for lunch or eat out.
I refuse to have a repeat of the incident where Marissa microwaved fish and stank up the entire building. It's bad for business.

A weak, unhinged chuckle left Sydney's mouth, causing the middle-aged man a few seats over to give her a strange look. She wanted to grab him and scream that ghosts existed, but instead she picked up her coffee and took a small sip. Her hand trembled, but she managed not to spill the coffee all over her shirt. Her head spun as she tried to grasp all the implications of what she'd just confirmed.

There was an afterlife, and apparently it had cell service.

Maybe doing this in a mall had been a bad idea. It meant too many witnesses to her mental breakdown. She pushed away questions about higher powers and the nature of the universe and instead just focused on texting. That was all she could handle.

Sydney

Okay, I'm convinced.
No one but Glenda could sound so strict and unreasonable.

Glenda

You're making me out to be the bad guy when I'm simply doing what it takes to keep my business afloat.

But if that makes you believe me, then fine.

Sydney

What do you want from me?
I hate to be blunt, but you're dead.
I can't help you.

Glenda

You can help find my killer.

Sydney

You don't remember who killed you??

Glenda

I remember footsteps behind me.

It was strange since everyone else had left, but I thought one of you had forgotten something and come back to get it.

I started to turn around, and there was an explosion of pain in my head.

I assume that's what killed me.

Sydney

Yeah, someone bashed your head in.
Sorry.
You really didn't see anything?

Glenda

No. That's why I need your help. I can't move on until I get justice.

Sydney
Why the heck not?

Glenda
I don't know. I just know you're supposed to help me. I can't explain why. You'll just have to take my word for it.

Oh no. Sydney had just started to accept that she was texting a ghost, and now that ghost wanted her to play Sherlock Holmes and solve a murder?

Scratch that. Comparing herself to Sherlock Holmes was a bit much. She was probably more like Inspector Gadget—except without all the cool gizmos, so just bumbling and clueless.

Sydney
I don't have to take your word for anything.
Why me? I'm not a detective.

Glenda
If you didn't cast a spell on me, then I don't know.
I'd say this is the work of a higher power, but I can't imagine why you of all people would be the one chosen to help me. There's certainly no shortage of better options.
But you're all I have.

Sydney
I don't know about this.

Glenda
This isn't a request.
You have to help me.

Sydney
I'm not your employee anymore, so I don't have to do anything.
Look, I'm not saying no. I just need time to think.

Glenda

While you're wasting time, the killer is probably covering their tracks!

Sydney

And I wouldn't even know where to start looking for them. Just give me some time. I'll text you back.

Glenda

You'd better.

Chapter 7

This can only end in tears

11:47
Faith
Can you come into work tomorrow?
I know it's going to be uncomfortable with what happened there, but I want to open back up.

Sydney
Yeah, I can come.

Faith
Thanks. I'll see you in the morning.

Sydney
Are you sure you want to be there? Marissa and I can handle the place if you need more time.

Faith
I need something to keep me busy, to be honest.
And I don't want to lose any more business. I have to keep the bakery going for Mom.

Sydney
I can understand that.
See you tomorrow then.

• • •

Sydney spent all morning and most of the afternoon at

the mall, trying to reclaim some semblance of a normal life. She treated herself to a few bath bombs at Lush, figuring that having a haunted phone entitled her to a relaxing bath at the very least. She bought some horror movie graphic tees, found a cute belly button ring with a charm shaped like a slice of cake, and ate a soft pretzel.

And she didn't get murdered by a ghost. All things considered, it had been a good trip to the mall.

She hit the grocery store on the way home and made a sheet pan recipe of chicken and vegetables for dinner. With a full stomach and a glass of wine, she finally felt ready to text back Glenda.

Sydney
Okay, I'm in.

Glenda
You certainly kept me waiting long enough.

Sydney
Sorry if it took me a few hours to get used to the idea that my boss's ghost is texting me from the afterlife and I have to find her killer.

Glenda
I've been telling you that since yesterday. You're the one who refused to believe me.

Sydney sighed. Less than a minute in, and she was already regretting it.

Sydney
Whatever. Let's start with the evening you were killed. What happened after I left?

Glenda
Nothing special. Faith and Marissa left shortly after you did. I

was balancing the register.

Sydney
Marissa left first, then Faith?

Glenda
Yes. How did you know?

Sydney
That's what Marissa told me. I just wanted to check. What happened next?

Glenda
I finished counting the money. The drawer was three cents short.

I opened the safe in my office to deposit everything, and that's when I heard the footsteps.

Sydney
Did you lock the doors after Faith left?

Glenda
Of course. For all the good it did me.

Sydney
You're absolutely sure?

Glenda
Yes! Don't treat me like I'm senile.

So much for Alex's theory that Glenda had left the door unlocked. Her sister had always been a hopeless optimist.

Sydney
Then it really was an employee.

Glenda
What do you mean?

Sydney
I overheard the police on Saturday. The door was unlocked. There was no sign of it being forced open. Whoever killed you must have had a key.

Glenda
Unbelievable.
Couldn't someone have picked the lock?

Sydney
Maybe.
But I don't know what you expect me to do if this was a professional thief. They've probably already skipped town.

Glenda
Thief?

Sydney
Oh yeah. All the money in your safe was stolen.

Glenda
What?!
How dare they! Sydney, you have to find the culprit. They need to pay for what they've done.

Sydney
Yeah, that's the idea.
Let's talk suspects. Besides you and me, Faith, Marissa, and Javier have keys, right?

Glenda
And Caleb. He never returned his after leaving. I was looking into getting the locks changed actually.

Sydney felt like a bug had just crawled down her throat. The possibility that Caleb could have done it had never crossed her mind. Sure, he was kind of a jerk sometimes, but a murderer?

Glenda

It was probably him! I'm sure he wanted the money, and he hates me—especially since I was going to fire him.

Sydney

You were? Why?

Never mind. I assume it's because he was late all the time and did super sloppy decorating work.

I still remember that Easter bunny cake that looked like a possessed goat.

Glenda

There's that, yes.

But didn't he tell you why he quit? I thought you two were dating.

Sydney

We broke up.

And no. I just assumed he got fed up with you hovering over him all the time when he worked.

Glenda

If I didn't, he would've eyeballed the ingredients and not properly measured anything.

And for your information, he quit because I caught him drinking in the bathroom.

He knew I was going to fire him.

Sydney

Seriously?

Glenda

He was halfway through a bottle of whiskey.

That dope. Sydney wanted to go over to his apartment

and smack him. She understood how working for Glenda could drive a person to drink, but he should have waited until after work hours like everybody else.

Sydney
He's like a factory of bad decisions.
Ugh, okay.
I don't think he's a killer, but he had motive and opportunity, so he's on the suspect list.
Let's move to Faith.

Glenda
My daughter isn't a suspect!

Sydney
We have to consider everyone who has a key no matter how much we don't like it.

Glenda
Then what about you? You have one.

Of course Sydney couldn't get haunted by a reasonable, appreciative ghost. No, she got stuck with Glenda.

Sydney
Why would I bother texting you if I'm the murderer?

Glenda
Maybe you want to torment me.

Sydney
If it was me, you're screwed, because I'm the only one you can contact.
And for the record, I didn't do it. I was at my sister's birthday party, and everyone there can confirm my alibi.

Glenda
You could be lying to me.

Sydney
I could, but there's nothing you can do about it if that's the case, so why don't we just work under the assumption that I'm innocent?

Glenda
Fine.

Huh. Sydney had never won so many arguments with Glenda when the woman had been alive. Should she feel guilty about abusing her power as the only person Glenda could contact?

Maybe later. She had interrogating to do.

Sydney
Good. Back to Faith.
It's possible that after years of getting bullied and dismissed by you, she finally snapped.

Glenda
I don't bully her.

Sydney
"You can handle something that simple without screwing it up, right?"
That's an exact quote from Saturday while you were refusing to even listen to her suggestions.

Glenda
You don't have children. I wouldn't expect you to understand.

Sydney
I understand that's a terrible way to talk to another person.

Glenda

But the money was stolen. Faith has no motive for that.

I pay her well, and my daughter-in-law works in purchasing for a big automotive company. They're comfortable financially.

Sydney

She could've taken it to cover her tracks.

Make it look like the motive was robbery and not revenge.

Glenda

This is absurd.

And insulting.

Sure, Sydney was the insulting one. If talking with Glenda was a drinking game and Sydney took a shot every time the woman insulted her, she'd die of alcohol poisoning within an hour.

Sydney

Look, I'm doubtful it's really her.

She seemed honestly distraught on Sunday, and she doesn't even like getting frosting on her hands, so I can't see her managing something as messy and bloody as murder.

I just think it's too soon to take her off the suspect list.

Glenda

All right.

Let's move on to Marissa—unless accusing my daughter is okay but suggesting your friend isn't?

Sydney took a deep breath. She needed more wine—or maybe less; she wasn't sure. Marissa had been her friend for so many years. In high school, she'd had the coolest collection of leather boots and always scored tickets to the best rock concerts. Teenage Sydney had idolized the older girl. Marissa had even been the one to tell her when Summertime Sweets had been hiring, so Sydney had her to thank for her job.

Sydney
No, we need to consider Marissa.
I don't want to think she's capable of something like this, but she does have a motive. She needs the money.
She has a lot of student-loan debt, and she's not the best at managing her finances.
Her family was well off, so she never had to worry about money before.
But if she needed cash, she could ask her parents. There's no reason to do something as desperate as robbery.

Glenda
We should still keep her on the list.

Sydney
Agreed.

Glenda
That leaves Javier.

Sydney
Yeah, I can't figure out what his motive would be.
I don't think he needs the money, and he's so chill. He seems to shrug it off whenever you're a jerk to him, so we can probably rule out the rage/revenge angle.
But he lied about where he was on Saturday.

Glenda
He wasn't at the auto repair shop?

Sydney
No, my sister said she saw him at the gas station Saturday morning.
I guess he could've been on his way to the shop, but it seems doubtful.

Glenda

And to think I trusted him.
He's normally so responsible.

Sydney

Right. So four suspects then.

Glenda

You should break into their homes while they're out and search for the murder weapon.

Sydney

Yeah…
Before I start doing stuff that could get me arrested, I think I'll just talk to them tomorrow.
I should be able to make it seem casual and find out who has an alibi or not.

Glenda

If you say so.
You can't screw this up, Sydney. I'm depending on you.
You don't want me to be stuck in this purgatory forever, do you?

Sydney

Since I'm the only one that you can text, and I can't block your number?
No. No, I do not.

Chapter 8

How not to solve a mystery

Sydney arrived at the bakery the next morning, relieved to see no flashing red and blue lights. Memories of the morning Glenda's body had been discovered were burned into her brain, and she wondered how long it would take before she could pull into the parking lot without feeling a shiver of fear.

She was a few minutes early, so she headed to the restaurant first. The door was open, the crew already at work. Sawdust covered the floor, power cords snaking across it to different pieces of equipment. Wooden frames stood where new walls weren't finished, but Sydney glimpsed dark brick and industrial lighting that hinted at something stylish and modern.

Logan spotted her and came over. He wore a flannel shirt and brown jacket, a little sweaty from hard labor but still somehow with perfect hair.

"You've been busy over here," Sydney said.

"Yeah, it's coming along. How are you doing?"

Her gaze dropped to the floor. "Okay, I guess. It's been… a weird few days."

At what point in a relationship did you tell someone you could send text messages to a ghost? Probably not until after the first date.

"I bet." He looked at her closely, making her wonder how much of the stress of the past few days showed on her face. "Is this the first time you've been back to the bakery since it happened?"

"Yeah."

"That's hard. I wish I could help."

Sydney shrugged. "I just gotta suck it up and get it over

with. What are you doing today?"

He gestured at the construction. "More of the same. And lunch with you, if you're interested."

"I'm interested." *Very, very interested.* "I get eleven to twelve o'clock off. There's a good Indian buffet across the street."

"Works for me," he said. "I'll come by at eleven."

It was nice to have something to look forward to besides a murder investigation and text messages from beyond the grave, but Sydney's good mood evaporated when she stepped into the bakery. She stared at the floor, searching for traces of bloodstains. The tile looked clean, but Glenda hadn't died there, had she? It must have happened in her office by the safe, and it would have been cleaned up by now, right?

Kendall, one of the part-time employees, manned the register. (She didn't have a key, so she wasn't a suspect. At least not unless she did something suspicious.) Sydney said good morning before clocking in. Faith was working at the computer in Glenda's office. Her face was pale, her eyes still red-rimmed. Sydney's determination to sneakily interrogate her vanished, and she said an awkward hello before going to start work on the day's catering orders.

Marissa came in a minute later, and again, Sydney found herself tongue-tied. She'd underestimated how hard it would be to treat her friends and coworkers as murder suspects.

"New jacket?" she asked in a pitiful attempt at small talk.

"Yeah," Marissa replied. "It was time for a change."

It was the only conversation they could manage. They worked in awkward silence for about fifteen minutes, the humming of mixers and clinking of cookware the only sounds.

Marissa glanced around and lowered her voice. "You thinking about the murder?"

"Yep," Sydney said. "You?"

"Can't stop no matter how hard I try. You…" Marissa

shuffled from foot to foot. "You were camping with Alex, right?"

Sydney looked up from the sugar she was melting to make caramel. "You think I'm a suspect?"

"Sorry. You must hate me. I just—"

"No," Sydney said quickly. "This is why we're friends. We're on the same wavelength. I've been thinking that about *everyone*. And yeah, Alex and like ten of her friends can vouch for me."

This was the perfect opportunity. Sydney would kick herself if she let it slip away. She gathered her courage.

"Were you…?"

"I was just with one person," Marissa said. "But yeah. I have an alibi."

"Who was it?"

She glanced away. "He's nobody. It was just a one-night kind of thing."

"Good for you. I hope he was a good time." Sydney rubbed her forehead. "I'm so stressed out from suspecting everyone."

"I know what you mean. I've gone over every little thing that happened on Saturday a thousand times." Marissa looked around the kitchen again to make sure no one could overhear. When she spoke, her voice was almost a whisper. "Do you think it's weird that Javier took off that day?"

If only Marissa knew how much Sydney had agonized over that question.

"Maybe," she said. "I've thought about it, but what's his motive?"

Marissa's eyes widened. "Didn't you hear? His wife got laid off last month."

"What?" Sydney set down the whisk in her hand. "I didn't know that."

"Yeah, I heard she's been temping but hasn't found anything permanent yet."

"Oh man."

Marissa nodded gravely. "Yeah. And with four kids to

take care of, he could be feeling the pressure…"

The sugar had melted. Sydney took the pot off the heat and added butter, whisking as she thought. Could Javier have lurked outside the bakery and snuck in after Faith left? Had he intended to kill Glenda, or had he just planned a burglary and been surprised by her presence inside?

"Then there's Faith…," Marissa said.

"You think she finally snapped?"

Marissa raised her eyebrows. "Could you blame her? But no, I was thinking I heard Glenda say something to her about a secret last week."

Interesting. "What kind of secret?"

"I don't know. They stopped talking when they saw me. It sounded like Faith has something she's not telling anyone though."

"Hmm."

That was just great. Sydney had been hoping to rule out suspects, but she was just finding more and more reasons why everyone might want Glenda dead.

"I guess I could be overreacting," Marissa said. "They might have been talking about something totally innocent like the secret ingredient in Glenda's bourbon cake."

Sydney snorted. "Pretty sure the only secret to that is lots of bourbon."

"But I've never been able to re-create it! Believe me, I've tried." Marissa's smile faded. "I guess I'll never know the secret now that Glenda's gone…"

"Yeah…"

With Glenda texting her from beyond the grave, it was hard to remember that the woman's life had ended. She would never be able to retire and travel or spend more time with her family. Someone had stolen that from her.

Sydney's phone buzzed. Speak of the devil.

Glenda
Any news?

Sydney angled her body away from Marissa so that her coworker couldn't see the screen.

Sydney

Nothing concrete.
Stop texting me during work. I don't want anyone to see a dead woman's name on my phone.

Glenda

I expect an update as soon as you clock out.

You'd think death might have made her less pushy. Sydney shook her head as she slipped her phone back into her apron pocket. Micromanaging Sydney was probably the only way Glenda could feel as if she had some control over the situation. Sydney should try to cut the woman some slack, seeing as she'd been murdered and all.

She couldn't help but imagine Glenda showing up to the pearly gates, gesturing wildly as she argued with Saint Peter. If dying hadn't changed the woman, nothing would.

The rest of the morning passed normally, no more big revelations about her coworkers having motives for murder. Sydney mulled things over as she mixed dough and piped frosting. Did Javier feel desperate enough for money that he would rob the bakery? And what secret did Faith have? Was it something worth killing over?

Sydney felt relieved Marissa had an alibi… Except she could be lying, couldn't she? Weren't detectives supposed to confirm a suspect's alibi? Sydney had no idea how to do that without the name of the guy Marissa had hooked up with. Marissa must have told the police his name—if she'd known it. If it had been a one-night stand, she might not have bothered to ask.

When Logan strolled into the bakery at eleven o'clock, Sydney felt some of the tension leave her shoulders. She needed a break from the thoughts running through her head.

"Be out in a second," she called, taking off her apron. "Just let me grab my purse."

He raised a hand in acknowledgment and then idly browsed the array of sweets on display.

"Who's that?" Marissa whispered, shooting him an appreciative look.

"Logan Kobayashi," Sydney answered. "He's the guy opening the new restaurant next door."

"Handsome *and* entrepreneurial. Sydney, you have all the luck."

She pulled on her coat. "You know I dated Caleb for two years, right?"

A bark of laughter left Marissa's mouth. "Point taken."

Logan offered to drive, but Sydney insisted on going separately in her own car. He seemed nice so far, but you never knew. She wanted an escape route in case he turned out to be a jerk or a serial killer or something.

Sydney took a deep breath when they walked in the door, savoring the scent of spices. Logan was already inside. He'd taken off his jacket, and with his sleeves rolled up, she caught a glimpse of a tattoo of rolling waves on his left arm and some kind of wing on his right. Her interest in him, already high, went up another notch, and she forced herself not to daydream about the rest of his body and what kind of ink might decorate it.

They chatted as they moved down the buffet table, loading up on different curries and naan. She learned that in addition to owning the restaurant next door, he was also the head chef. Cooking immediately gave them something in common to talk about.

"So," Logan said as they sat down and started eating. "Self-taught or culinary school?"

"Self-taught," she said. "I got my associate's in business actually. Baking was a hobby, and I started working at Summertime Sweets part-time to pay for school. It kind of turned into my career accidentally, but it worked out for the best. I love making weird cakes."

"Favorite one you ever made?"

"Hmm…" Sydney took a bite of chicken vindaloo as she considered. "This tiered red velvet cake with a realistic human heart on top made from fondant and gooey blood dripping down the sides. I'm a huge horror fan."

He glanced her over, his mouth forming a grin. "Yeah, I get that vibe from you."

"Ha." And she wasn't even wearing her *Friday the 13th* T-shirt. "So what about you? How'd you get into cooking?"

She hadn't realized he'd been leaning forward until he slumped back, evidently not as interested in talking about himself as he was her. "I used to help my grandma in the kitchen. Didn't think of making a career of it until later."

"Same question then. Self-taught or culinary school?"

"Culinary school. It took a while, but I eventually found a program that would take me. I spent my high school years getting into trouble, so my grades weren't the best."

She tried to imagine him in his teens. "You were a little rebel, huh?"

He looked away. "Something like that."

"Well, you seem to have grown into a responsible member of society."

He smirked. "Is that a compliment or an insult?"

"A compliment—mostly." She smirked right back. "Teenage me wanted to be a rock star. She'd probably be terribly disappointed to learn she becomes a baker, but it's a good, steady job."

He tore off a piece of naan and dipped it in his curry, looking thoughtful as he chewed. "I think I was nineteen when I decided I wanted to open my own restaurant."

"Wow." Her fork hovered in front of her mouth for a second. "You weren't kidding when you said you've been working toward this for a decade."

"I started out busing tables to pay for school, moved into the kitchen once I'd gotten my degree. I've spent the past six years working to learn the business, pay off my student loans, and save up enough to start my own restaurant. I'm…" He rubbed his face. "Let's just say I'm hoping it's successful."

Sydney took a moment to absorb all that, impressed. He had a goal and wasn't afraid to put in the hard work to reach it. She didn't want to constantly compare him to Caleb, but… He was pretty much the exact opposite of Caleb.

She raised her water in a toast. "To success then."

Their glasses clinked together lightly.

"To success," he said.

• • •

Nothing noteworthy happened that afternoon except a rainstorm. Glenda texted her at 4:01 to ask what she'd learned, but Sydney needed a few more minutes to wrap things up at the bakery. She clocked out at five after four and then headed for the door, wishing she had an umbrella.

Kendall hovered by the door, rubbing her arms nervously. A petite Black girl, she worked part-time to help pay her college tuition.

"Hey," she said. "I know it's the middle of the afternoon, but… Would you mind walking me to my car? I'll wait until I see you get into yours before driving off."

Sydney looked out the window. The rain clouds had turned the afternoon sunlight into a darkness that rivaled the night. Rain poured down in sheets, half the parking lot flooded. Not a single soul was in sight, everyone probably staying indoors wherever possible. It looked desolate and creepy, the perfect place for Glenda's killer to strike.

"Yeah, no problem." Sydney turned to where Marissa and Faith were getting ready to go. "We should probably all use the buddy system."

Faith swallowed, her face paling. "That's a good idea."

"I'm almost ready, Faith," Marissa said. "Just give me a second, and we can walk out together."

This sucks, Sydney thought as she stepped out the door. How long would fear dominate their actions like this?

Would things ever get back to normal?

Not until you figure out who murdered Glenda, said a voice in the back of her head.

"I need to stop by next door real quick," Sydney told Kendall. "It'll only take a second."

Kendall didn't object, and Sydney popped inside the restaurant to say goodbye to Logan.

"Don't work too late," she told him.

He winked. "No promises."

"Then be careful," she said. "With what happened to Glenda…"

His expression sobered. "I'll stay alert. You be careful too."

Sydney and Kendall dashed through the rain, the ice-cold water soaking them instantly. She escorted Kendall to her car and then raced to her own, shivering as she closed the door behind her.

She waved as Kendall drove off, starting the car and turning up the heat. Then she pulled out her phone to update Glenda.

Sydney

Marissa says she has an alibi, but since it's a one-night stand, I don't know how I could track down the guy to check. And now that I think about it, even if she's telling the truth, she could have killed you and then gone to meet the guy. You said it happened not long after we left, right?

Glenda

That's right. I'd guess about ten minutes. So maybe around 4:15.

Sydney

That soon? Then my alibi at the campground is worthless. I bet the police suspect me too.

Glenda

Find the real killer, and your problem is solved.

Oh sure. Because it was that easy. Sydney thought back to her conversation with the officer who'd interviewed her on the morning after the murder. He hadn't seemed accusing, and no one had called her for a follow-up interview since then. Did that mean they'd ruled her out as a suspect? Or were they quietly building evidence against her before bringing her in?

Glenda
What about Javier?

Sydney's fear pulled her thoughts on a tangent like a dog on a leash, yanking around its owner. She reined it in with difficulty. Glenda might be oversimplifying things, but she was right: Sydney should focus on finding the real killer.

Sydney
He wasn't on the schedule today. I'll talk to him later. Marissa said his wife lost her job recently though, so it turns out he might have a motive after all.

Glenda
I find it hard to believe he's the killer.
Caleb, on the other hand, seems all too likely. Have you talked to him yet?

Sydney
I'll text him when I get home.

Movement caught her eye through her rain-streaked windshield. Faith and Marissa sprinted through the parking lot, heads ducked to shield themselves from the rain. Sydney felt relieved as they both entered their cars safely. She'd been the one to suggest the buddy system, but on second thought, what good would that do when one of the buddies might be the murderer?

Sydney
Marissa said something else. Apparently you and Faith were talking about a secret of hers the other week. What's that about?

Glenda
Nothing. It's not relevant.

Sydney glared at the screen—for all the good it did her. It wasn't like Glenda could see her face. If text messages worked in the afterlife, then why not video calls?

Sydney
Why don't you let me be the judge of that?

Glenda
It's none of your business, Sydney.

Sydney
You made it my business when you asked me to find the killer. This is going to be hard enough without you keeping information from me.
I need to know everything.

Glenda
Trust me when I say it's not important.
You should be looking into Marissa's and Caleb's alibis, not poking your nose into my family's private business.

Sydney
Forget it. You're such a pain.

Glenda
Forget what? You're still going to investigate, aren't you?
You need to talk to Caleb.

Sydney
I'll talk to him.
Maybe I'll tell you what he says.
You know, if I deem it relevant.

Glenda
Now you're just being difficult for no reason.
I expect you to report every detail of what he says.

4:19
Glenda
Sydney?

Chapter 9

Lies, probably

Sydney never took her commute for granted. She lived on the west side of Beaverfield, and Summertime Sweets stood on the easternmost border, but it still only took her twenty minutes to cross town, barring traffic accidents or snow-related slowdowns. She pulled into her apartment complex around half past four. It was a nice place, comprising three-story brick buildings built about twenty years earlier but still in good condition. The grounds had small ponds that attracted flocks of geese, and while it didn't have a gym, there was a pool near the leasing office.

Given that Beaverfield only had pool weather three months out of the year, Sydney would have preferred a gym.

She kicked off her shoes and tossed her coat onto a chair. Glancing at her wine rack, she decided instead on a cup of tea. Settling on the couch and inhaling the spicy scent of chai, she texted Caleb.

Sydney
Hey, did you hear about Glenda?

Caleb
Yeah. People are sick.
The whole thing is seriously messed up.

Sydney
I know, right?
I showed up to work not long after Faith found the body. It was awful. Cops were everywhere.

Caleb
Yeah, they came to interview me.
Must've heard I quit last week.

Sydney blew on her hot tea and tried to picture Caleb getting angry enough to attack Glenda. She just couldn't see it. Caleb had never shown a temper during the years she'd dated him. He didn't care about anything enough to get riled up.

On the other hand, Caleb thinking that stealing from the safe would be a quick and easy way to get cash? That seemed more likely. Had he expected the bakery to be empty? He should have known better so soon after four o'clock. He had a key; he could sneak inside in the middle of the night if he wanted to. Then again, it wouldn't be the first time he'd failed to think something through.

Sydney
What'd they say?

Caleb
Lots of stuff. Was I angry with her when I quit, did she have any enemies—that kind of thing.

Sydney
They asked me the same thing.
I said she made more enemies than she did sprinkled cupcakes.

Caleb
Lol. For real.

Sydney
Do you have an alibi?

Caleb
Why are you asking?

Sydney
I'm just asking.

Caleb
You think I did it?

Sydney considered how to respond and decided to go with honesty.

Sydney
I think her murder would've taken careful planning, perfect timing, and keeping cool under pressure.
So no, I don't think you did it.

Caleb
Good, because I didn't.
And for the record, I have an alibi.

Sydney
So what is it?

Caleb
This is why we broke up. You're almost as pushy as Glenda sometimes.

Sydney stared at the screen, waiting for the anger that usually flared when he insulted her. All she felt was mild annoyance. She supposed his words didn't sting as much since they'd broken up and she'd moved on.

She had moved on, hadn't she? She was only texting him as part of her investigation. They were done. She'd sworn it. Except she'd done that three times before and always ended up getting back together with him. He was familiar and risk-free, and they could have fun together as long as she didn't think about their relationship too much.

Sydney
I thought it was because I'm an "abrasive ice queen."
Isn't that what you called me?

Caleb
You know I didn't mean it, babe.

Sydney
Yeah, sure.
So who do you think killed Glenda?

Caleb
Probably just some random psychopath.
Or maybe Faith.
Glenda only called her useless and incompetent like three times a day.

Sydney
It's possible.

Caleb
Hey. You be careful at the bakery, okay?
It's obviously not safe.

Sydney
Yeah. I will.

Her tea had cooled down enough to drink, so she took a slow sip. Their conversation hadn't achieved anything. If Caleb refused to give details about his alibi, she had no way of forcing him. She could only hope he'd told the police the truth, and they'd verified what he'd said.

Because the police hopefully knew what they were doing; Sydney didn't have a clue. Groaning, she sank deeper into the couch cushions. What did she think she was playing at trying to solve a murder? Why the heck did her phone have a connection to the afterlife? Was it some kind of cosmic joke? What did it mean?

Existential dread clawed at her throat. She took another sip of tea and tried to calm down. It didn't work, so she went into the kitchen to get an early start on dinner. Cooking always soothed her when she felt stressed, and Alex would be coming over tonight, so Sydney might as well get started.

They ate together once a week and took turns hosting, a tradition they'd implemented after they'd both graduated and found themselves so busy that they rarely saw each other despite living in the same town. Sydney tended to cook something healthy and balanced in an attempt to get some nutrients into her sister's system since Alex lived on takeout and microwave dinners. She usually ordered out when it was her turn to host.

It was Sydney's fault. The first time Alex had tried to cook for her, she'd boiled spaghetti and somehow set the noodles on fire. Sydney had laughed so hard that Alex probably felt too embarrassed to try again.

Tonight Sydney needed comfort food, and that meant pizza. She chopped up a head of cauliflower and shredded it in the blender, mixing it with eggs, cheese, and herbs to make the crust. While it baked in the oven, she grabbed some hot Italian sausage for the topping. The recipe took more time and effort than she usually felt like putting in after work, but she'd wanted a distraction, so it was perfect.

Ten minutes were left on the oven timer when her phone buzzed.

Logan

I had a good time at lunch today. You up for going out again tomorrow?

Sydney wiped the bits of food from her fingers before typing a reply.

Sydney
Sure.
Though you should know that there are only two good lunch places around.
That Indian buffet and an Italian deli down the street.

Logan
The deli it is then.

Sydney wouldn't have made pizza if she'd known she would be eating Italian again tomorrow, but oh well. Lunch would still be delicious, and she couldn't ask for better company.

Sydney
I'm looking forward to the meatball sub already.
Are you still at the restaurant?

Logan
Just finishing up a few things.

Sydney
Go home and get some rest so you don't pass out face-first into the meatballs tomorrow.

Logan
Ha.
Yes ma'am.

Sydney started slicing peppers before adding them to the skillet. He was still interested—awesome. She'd thought their lunch date had gone well, but it was nice to get confirmation. She felt a little flutter in her stomach as she thought about him.

Don't get too excited, she warned herself. *You've only had one date.* Logan could still turn out to be a creep, though she hoped not. For one thing, she wouldn't be able to avoid him with his restaurant right next to the bakery. That could get awkward fast. She pictured herself scanning the parking lot from the window and dashing to her car when the coast was clear—or running into him at the dumpster again and making painful, awkward small talk.

Maybe she shouldn't date people she worked near. Or with. Just look at Caleb.

But it was too late now. She'd just have to see this bad idea through to the end. She was still smiling to herself when she heard the click of someone unlocking her front door. Panic shot through her for a second—there was a murderer on the loose—before she realized it was just Alex.

"How's it going?" Sydney asked.

Alex groaned in response. She slumped down the hallway and kicked off her shoes before unzipping her jacket, a scowl on her pretty face. She wore a cream-colored sweater that looked extremely soft and jeans with holes torn artfully in the knees, her cheeks red from the cold outside.

"All these websites want me to write for exposure." She threw up her hands. "Exposure! I can't pay my bills with that. What kind of idiots expect people to work for free?"

"Entitled ones," Sydney replied, taking down two plates from the cabinet.

Alex flopped down on the couch and crossed her arms. "I referred them to the rates on my website. I'll probably never hear from them again."

"Good riddance," Sydney said.

Alex grunted. She glared at the blank TV screen in front of her for several seconds like it had personally insulted her. Then she snapped out of her funk and looked over at the kitchen.

"Oh hey. How was your first day back at work?"

The timer beeped. Sydney opened the oven, stepping back as heat surged out, and carefully removed the pizza. "Bad news: suspecting all your coworkers of murder doesn't exactly make a relaxing work environment. Good news: I had a nice lunch date."

"Boo for the murder stuff and yay for the lunch date." Her eyes narrowed. "Wait. Was it with Caleb?"

"No, not Caleb."

"A guy who's not Caleb?" Alex sped toward the kitchen. "I like him already. Tell me everything."

"Very funny." Sydney pulled out her pizza cutter from the drawer and got to work. "His name's Logan. He's a chef opening a restaurant next to the bakery. He's got nice tattoos and an impressive sarcastic streak when he's angry."

Alex, who'd been staring at the pizza and visibly salivating, looked up sharply. "When he's angry? Why was this guy angry at you?"

"Not at me. At Glenda."

Alex's blond eyebrows shot up. "At your boss who was just murdered? Doesn't that seem a little sketchy to you?"

"It's not like that." Sydney handed her a plate, trying to ignore the tug of worry in her stomach. Logan couldn't have had anything to do with Glenda's death. He didn't have a motive.

She remembered their argument on the sidewalk the morning of the murder and felt her stomach twist up further.

"Glenda was being her usual unreasonable self," Sydney said firmly. "He just stood his ground."

Alex gave her a dubious look but then scooped up a slice of pizza. "But you'll be careful, right? Don't go anywhere with him that's not public until you're sure."

"I won't. I usually stick to public places for the first few dates anyway. And I bought pepper spray. I'm keeping it in my purse."

"Good." Alex carried her plate to the kitchen table. "I hope the killer gets caught soon. I'll feel a lot safer when they're arrested."

Reaching for her own slice of pizza, Sydney's hand froze a few inches from the pan. Should she tell Alex about her own investigation? She didn't usually keep secrets from her sister—especially not about huge things like this. But what was she supposed to say? *I'm getting texts from Glenda's ghost. If you've ever wondered about life after death, then good news!*

Alex would never believe her. Sydney could show her the texts, but Alex didn't know Glenda like Sydney did. She would think Sydney had fallen for a scam, that the texter was a crook.

And what if she *did* believe her? Did Sydney want to share all the worry and fear she'd felt since this mess started? Her sister didn't need that on her shoulders.

"Yeah," Sydney said finally. "Me too."

She sat down at the table and steered the rest of their conversation away from murder and death.

• • •

Alex went home after dinner, and Sydney cleaned up before settling on the couch with a horror novel. Considering what was going on in her actual life, she didn't want to read about ghosts or murderers, so she picked one about vampires and was about five chapters in when her phone buzzed on top of the coffee table.

Sydney huffed and set aside her e-reader. Couldn't Glenda give her *one* evening to herself? But when she glanced at the screen, it wasn't Glenda's name on it.

Javier
Hey, I've got a huge favor to ask.

Javier: one of the two suspects Sydney hadn't talked to in person yet. And she hated thinking of him like that—as a potential criminal instead of a good friend. Sydney was never going to win a Miss Congeniality award, but it made her feel like even more of a jerk than usual.

Javier
I know tomorrow's your day off and this is short notice, but would you be able to switch shifts with me? You take Thursday, and I'll take

Friday?

My youngest needs to go to the doctor's tomorrow morning, and I'm the only one who can take him.

Sydney

Is he okay?

Javier

Looks like an ear infection.

Sydney

Poor kid.

I can switch, but you've got to answer a question for me first.

Javier

Okay…?

Sydney

Where were you on Saturday?

Javier

What do you mean?

Sydney

You said your car broke down, which is weird since you were seen filling it up at the gas station that morning.

There. That kept Alex's name out of it in case he was the murderer and wanted to cover his tracks. Of course, if that was the case, then Sydney had just painted a target on her own back by hinting that she suspected him. But that was what her pepper spray was for.

Javier

You're not asking me because you think I'm involved in the murder, are you?

And that's why she liked Javier. He was a straightforward, honest guy. She gave him truthfulness in return.

Sydney
I don't know. You tell me.
Glenda's dead and I'm freaking out.

Javier
I'm freaking too.
My brother-in-law's on the force, and I've been calling him for updates at least twice a day.

Sydney
What did he say?

Javier
Just that they're following leads and to be patient as they investigate.

Sydney
Are they investigating you?

Javier
It's not like that.

He typed, and Sydney had to remind herself to breathe as she waited for him to finish.

Javier
Look, I'll tell you, but you have to promise not to say anything to Faith.
I should be the one to tell her.

Okay, that was suspicious as all get-out, but Javier wouldn't confess to murder in a text message, would he? Maybe he wasn't the killer, but he knew something about the murder and had told the police.

Sydney
I can't promise anything until I know what you're going to say.

Javier
Yeah, all right.
So you caught me. My car didn't break down.
I just told Glenda that because I didn't want her to know I was going to a job interview.

Sydney's head bowed forward, and she felt like she'd just finished a 10K run. She couldn't decide whether she felt more relieved Javier hadn't done anything suspicious or disappointed she was no closer to solving the mystery.

Sydney
Okay.
Bit of a roller coaster of emotions right now.
That's a big relief, and of course I won't tell Faith.
Sad you're leaving the bakery though.

Javier
Well, I haven't heard back yet, so I don't know if I'm really going anywhere.
But yeah. It's a pastry chef position at a restaurant in Ann Arbor.
Not looking forward to the commute, and I don't want to leave Summertime Sweets.
But Felicia's job had great benefits. If she can't find something similar soon, I'll need a full-time position for the health insurance.
I asked Glenda about going full time at the bakery first, but she said that would make us overstaffed or something.

Sydney
I'm sorry. That really sucks.

Javier
Yeah. I'll feel bad about quitting on Faith after everything that's happened, but I need to think about my family.

Sydney
Of course you do.
As bummed as I'll be to see you go, I'm crossing my fingers you get the new job.

Javier
Thanks, Sydney.

Sydney leaned back, glad she could cross Javier off the suspect list (once she confirmed he wasn't lying anyway, which would be easy enough if he got the job and gave Faith two weeks' notice). But if he hadn't killed Glenda, then Faith, Marissa, or Caleb must have done it, and Sydney didn't like those possibilities at all.

Sighing, she raised her phone to update Glenda.

Chapter 10

The truth hurts

At the bakery the next day, Sydney and Marissa stood beside each other at one of the big tables in the kitchen. The table had a large piece of paper spread across its surface and were sketching out designs for a wedding cake.

Faith had been the one to meet with the bride and groom, and judging by the worry lines that had formed on her face as she described their wishes to Sydney and Marissa, it had been a stressful meeting. The happy couple wanted an elaborate chandelier cake: four tiers tall, decorated with crystal designs, and hanging upside down from a stand. It was going to be huge, heavy, and very difficult to pull off.

"So why couldn't Javier come in today?" Marissa asked.

"Bringing his sick kid to the doctor," Sydney answered.

Marissa scribbled some notes about ingredients on the bottom of the paper. "Hmm."

"For what it's worth, he told me his alibi for Saturday, and I believe him."

Marissa looked up. "What was he doing?"

Sydney put a finger over her lips. "I'm sworn to secrecy for now, but you'll probably find out soon."

"Interesting…" Marissa looked furtively toward the office where Faith was working. "So if he didn't do it, that leaves Faith."

And you, Sydney thought.

"And Caleb," Sydney said aloud. "He didn't ever return his key. He says he has an alibi, but he was pretty cagey about it."

She sketched a few designs down the side of the cake,

wishing she could figure out a way to confirm her friend's alibi. She wanted to share everything she'd learned in her investigation. Marissa would be a perfect sounding board; she knew everyone at the bakery just as well as Sydney did, and she was hard to faze. Sydney wondered how she'd handle learning Glenda was a ghost though.

Marissa labeled the color of each cake layer. "It can't be Caleb," she said absently.

"Why not?"

Marissa's hand froze, leaving the *t* in *white* uncrossed. "Oh. Um…"

She stared down at the sketch, not meeting Sydney's eyes.

"What?" Sydney asked, getting a bad feeling.

Marissa shuffled her feet. The industrial refrigerator hummed, and a steady sloshing came from the dishwasher. From the front of the store, Kendall's voice was vaguely audible as she described their different cupcakes to a customer. The office door was firmly closed, giving no sign of what Faith was doing inside. She could be balancing the books, crying her eyes out, or plotting another murder. Sydney and Marissa were completely alone.

"I know he didn't do it," Marissa said finally. "I'm his alibi. He's mine too. I went over to his place right after work."

The pencil slipped from Sydney's hand and hit the table. She opened her mouth but couldn't think of what to say.

"I'm sorry," Marissa said quickly. "I was going to tell you. It wasn't anything serious. I don't even like him all that much. And you guys broke up, so it's no big deal, right?"

Sydney's mind spun. She didn't know how she felt, much less how to put it into words. Marissa and Caleb? Sydney had never even considered the possibility—mostly because Caleb had nicknamed her Bossy Britches, and she couldn't speak to him for two minutes without scoffing and rolling her eyes at what he said.

The two of them had hooked up? And in the days since

it had happened, neither had mentioned it to Sydney?

Luckily, one of the ovens picked that moment to start beeping.

"I'll get it," Sydney said, and rushed away.

• • •

Later, Sydney took out the trash to the dumpster in the back. The sun shone mockingly overhead in a clear blue sky, and a couple of fat gray squirrels darted across the dead grass on the other side of the fence. Sydney wanted a dark, gloomy sky to match her mood. Maybe some light rain. She had a heavy black umbrella that she could mope under and achieve a perfect melancholy aesthetic. The weather just didn't cooperate when she needed it.

It was chilly out, making her regret not putting on a jacket, but she didn't go inside right away. She leaned against the side of the building and pulled out her phone.

Sydney
It's not Marissa or Caleb.

Glenda
Are you sure?

Sydney
They have an alibi.

Glenda
It had better be an airtight one. I find the two of them the most suspicious out of everyone.

Sydney's thumbs hesitated over the screen, her glossy black nail polish gleaming in the sunlight. She really didn't want to share this with Glenda of all people, but it related to her murder; she had a right to know.

Sydney
Marissa went to his apartment after work.
He lives like three minutes away. You could walk there from the bakery. I doubt either of them would have time to murder you and clean themselves up before seeing each other.

It took a moment for Glenda to type her reply, and Sydney felt her face heat in humiliation. For once, she was glad they could only converse through text messages. Saying it in person would have been ten times worse.

Glenda
I'm sorry, Sydney.
I know you and Marissa are close.
Though quite frankly I don't know what you ever saw in Caleb.

Sydney stared at the screen, throat tight. She almost wished Glenda had callously brushed off her feelings as usual. Her sympathy hit with an even stronger sting.

Glenda
You're better off without them. That's what I learned when Faith's father left me.
He shot down all my ideas of becoming a baker—didn't think I could cut it.
Once he was gone, I was free to do what I wanted.
I found success, and so will you.

Sydney swallowed. Her best friend had slept with her ex-boyfriend, and now Sydney was having a touching moment with the ghost of her grouchy boss. What was the world coming to?

Sydney
Thanks.
And I hate to ask, but Javier, Marissa, and Caleb are pretty much ruled out now, so that leaves Faith.

What's her secret? I know you said it's not relevant, but I would feel a lot better knowing.

Glenda must have hesitated, because it took her thirty seconds to reply.

Glenda
Oh, all right. But you have to promise not to tell anyone.

Sydney
Sure.

Glenda
I'm serious. If this gets out, it could ruin the bakery.

Sydney
I promise I won't say anything.

Glenda
You'd better not. I don't know what the consequences are for breaking a promise to a dead person, but I'm sure it's something bad.

Nothing more came for several moments, and Sydney pictured Glenda standing in the empty, foggy purgatory she'd described as she prepared to spill her daughter's dark secret. What on Earth could Faith have done that would ruin the bakery if it got out? Had she stolen someone else's recipe? Baked something that gave a customer food poisoning?

Faith was harmless—a bit of a pushover honestly. Her biggest vice was overusing colored highlighters when she printed out everyone's schedule for the week.

Glenda
She has a gluten allergy.

Sydney waited for more, for some horrible scandal

related to the allergy, but nothing came. That was it, she realized. That was the secret.

"Are you serious?"

The words burst from her mouth, startling the nearby squirrels and sending them scampering away.

Sydney
That's all?

Glenda
I told you it wasn't important.

Sydney
But you just said it could ruin the bakery. You swore me to secrecy.

Glenda
Of course I did. What if people find out?
Who's going to want a cake from a gluten intolerant baker? They'll think we're some hippie bakery that makes tofu cakes and hemp brownies.

Sydney's mouth hung open as she stared at the screen.

Sydney
That is wrong on so many levels that I don't even know where to start.
I'll just say thank you for telling me.

Glenda
Where does that leave us on suspects?

Sydney
I don't know.
I'll keep thinking. Hopefully something will come to me.
I should get back to work.

She went back inside, her mind racing. If it wasn't Marissa or Caleb… Had Javier lied about the job interview? Sydney supposed she could ask him the name of the company and call them to double-check, but some weirdo questioning them about the whereabouts of one of their candidates would probably cost Javier the job before he even got it. Nobody would want an employee who attracted that kind of attention.

She wondered if Faith had an alibi. Just because her big secret was a huge bust didn't mean she hadn't finally snapped under the pressure of her mother's criticism and killed her. Sydney would have to find a way to subtly ask her about what she'd done after leaving the bakery that night. She would have to be careful about how she phrased it. If Faith was innocent, Sydney didn't want to hurt her any more than she'd been already.

Marissa was impossible to avoid, but she and Sydney only spoke about work stuff all morning, pretending nothing had happened. Sydney didn't have the time or energy to deal with the damage to their friendship on top of hunting down a murderer. She watched Faith as her attempt to quickly tidy up the fridge led to a massive organization project that involved alphabetizing the spice rack and futilely trying to track down a missing rolling pin. Sydney couldn't imagine her killing a person.

At eleven o'clock, Sydney walked outside and waited on the sidewalk for Logan.

"How was your morning?" he asked, coming out of the restaurant.

"Ugh," she replied.

He chuckled. "That bad?"

She had no intention of bringing up her ex-boyfriend—especially not in a way that implied she felt upset someone else had slept with him. She wasn't—not exactly. She couldn't muster up any feelings about Caleb. She was done with him. He could hook up with whomever he wanted.

But Marissa… Shouldn't a woman wait longer than a

week after her best friend's breakup to sleep with her ex? And you've got to check with the friend first. It was an unwritten rule. Sisters before misters.

"Just… workplace drama," she said.

"Ah." His face took on an appropriately solemn expression. "The only thing worse than that is family drama. Managing people is definitely the aspect of the restaurant business that I'm least looking forward to."

"Yeah. People are the worst. How about you? Good morning?"

"Not bad," he said. "A little scary."

Scary? Sydney instantly tensed. Had something else happened that she hadn't heard about? Another murder? An attempted break-in?

"What do you mean?" she asked.

"Remember when you said the most violence we get in this town is angry geese? I ran into a gang of them this morning on my way to the car. There were a dozen of them, and they were *hissing.*" He shuddered. "I was about ten seconds away from handing over my wallet and begging them to spare my life."

Sydney laughed.

Logan allowed himself a small, self-satisfied sort of smile, and she realized he'd only said that to cheer her up. A warm, floaty feeling enveloped her.

"To the deli?" she asked.

"Lead the way."

She turned to step off the sidewalk and spotted two police officers coming their way. She inhaled sharply, and Logan went still beside her. Were they coming to tell Faith they'd found Glenda's killer? Or had they uncovered evidence that Faith was the one who'd murdered her?

But they didn't go inside the bakery. They headed straight for Sydney and Logan.

Oh no, Sydney thought. *They think I did it.*

It was about an hour's drive from the bakery to the campground. Sydney had been on the road with no witnesses at the time of Glenda's death. Had anyone at Alex's party been able to confirm the exact time Sydney arrived? Did the police suspect she'd waited in the parking lot for her coworkers to leave and then snuck back inside to kill Glenda?

Sydney's empty stomach tossed nauseatingly. Maybe they just had more questions. But what if they arrested her? She couldn't find the real killer if she was behind bars. And what in the world would they think if they took her phone and looked at her text history?

The cops stopped right in front of them, and Sydney felt her knees tremble.

"Logan Kobayashi?" asked the officer on the right.

The muscles of Logan's face twitched, but then he hid his reaction with a carefully blank expression. "Yes…?"

"You're under arrest."

Chapter 11

Everything is awful

Sydney never made it to the deli. She stood on the sidewalk for several seconds after the cops took Logan away, and then she went back inside the bakery. Marissa had been watching through the window and rushed over to her.

"Holy cow," Marissa said. "Did they arrest him for what I think they arrested him for?"

Sydney nodded numbly.

"I can't believe it." Marissa craned her neck to look out the window again, though the cop car had already driven away. "I didn't suspect him at all."

Faith came out of her office, and Marissa immediately hurried over to tell her what had happened. Sydney couldn't take it. She made for the front door but then stopped when she saw people outside. Desperate for privacy, she practically ran through the kitchen and burst out the back door. It was empty behind the building, just her and the dumpster. A couple of food wrappers blew across the pavement like tumbleweeds in the desert.

She rubbed her face and just focused on breathing for a few minutes. When her lungs didn't feel like they were getting crushed under the weight of a car anymore, she tried to think. What should she do? Go down to the police station and tell them Logan was innocent? They wouldn't believe her. She didn't even know why they suspected him. How could she find out? She didn't know any cops.

Javier.

Her phone nearly dropped from her clammy fingers as she pulled it out of her purse and called him.

"What's up?" he asked.

"Your brother-in-law's a cop, right? Did you hear anything about the arrest today?"

"Uh, no. Why? What's going on?"

Sydney wanted to cry. "You know Logan Kobayashi, the chef from next door? They arrested him."

"For Glenda's murder? No way. He seemed so nice."

"He is nice!" Sydney's voice echoed off the back of the building. She took a deep breath and tried to calm down. "I don't think he did it. Can you find out what evidence they have and what they're charging him with?"

"I don't know… My bro's not supposed to talk to me about the investigation."

"Please?" she pleaded. "I really think Logan's innocent."

Javier exhaled noisily into the phone speaker. "I'll try. No promises though."

"Thank you."

They said goodbye, and Sydney paced up and down the asphalt. What now? She couldn't just sit around and wait.

Why did the police suspect Logan of murder? What was their evidence? Had the killer framed him? Sydney needed to find the truth fast and clear his name, but how? Her investigation had hit a brick wall. She'd gone from feeling suspicious of all her coworkers to not having one good suspect.

Unless Logan really *had* done it.

She shook her head. No. He had no motive. It couldn't have been him.

Had she gone on a lunch date with a murderer?

She needed to get to the bottom of this. She texted Glenda.

Sydney
Tell me everything you remember from the night you died.

Glenda
I already did.
I've been over it a thousand times in my head. I don't remember

anything new.
Why?

Sydney
Logan's been arrested.

Glenda
Who?

Sydney groaned. How could she not know his name after shouting at him for so long?

Sydney
The man opening the restaurant next door. The one you were yelling at about the construction noise.

Glenda
He killed me?
I should have known. He was so rude and unreasonable. I thought he was an unsavory character from the start. You should always trust your instincts on these things.
He probably did it so I wouldn't complain to the landlord about him.

Sydney
That's a terrible motive.
Why would he risk murdering someone over something so minor?

Glenda
People have killed for less, I'm sure.
Or he killed me for the money. He's starting a business, and that isn't cheap—believe me.

Oh fudge. That was actually a halfway decent motive. Sydney felt dizzy.

Sydney
But how did he get inside? He doesn't have a key.

Glenda
Maybe he stole one. Or he could have picked the lock.
The details aren't important. What matters is that the killer has been caught and it wasn't anyone in the bakery.

Sydney
I don't know.
I don't think it was him.

Glenda
How can you be so sure? You don't even know him.

Sydney
I know him. We've been texting.
We went on a lunch date.

Glenda
Is that supposed to convince me? You thought Caleb was boyfriend material. Your taste in men is obviously awful.

Sydney clenched her phone, resisting the urge to chuck it in the dumpster.

Sydney
Fine. I don't know why I thought you would help.

Glenda
And what is that supposed to mean?

Sydney
I've been busting my butt for you the past couple of days. The least you could do is give me a little support.
But why would I think you'd do something like that? You never showed me or anyone else at the bakery any appreciation.

You're a rude, overbearing bully, and dying hasn't changed you at all.

Glenda

You're the one being rude.

I'm your boss. I have a business to run. I don't have time to worry about everyone's fragile feelings.

Sydney

But you're perfectly polite to the customers.

You're only awful when you can get away with it—to people like your daughter and your employees.

Every single person in the bakery could have plausibly murdered you in revenge for how you treated them. That's screwed up, Glenda.

Glenda

If that's how you feel, then I'm not sure why you're even texting me.

Sydney

I don't know either.

• • •

Sydney made it through the rest of the workday in a haze. She had to toss a batch of cookies when she forgot to add baking soda and they came out of the oven as dense as hockey pucks, and a ramekin shattered on the floor when it slipped from her jittery hands. Marissa and Faith shot her glances whenever they thought she wasn't looking but didn't say anything.

At home, Sydney paced the length of her apartment. She had the TV on, waiting for the local news to come on at five in case they mentioned anything about the arrest. She hoped they didn't release Logan's name; getting accused of murder wouldn't exactly help the publicity around his restaurant's opening.

She kept going through her list of suspects and alibis, trying to find something she had missed. It had to be Faith, right? She was the only one not accounted for. But how could Sydney prove it? She might try to search Glenda's old office when Faith went on her lunch break, but the police had surely covered every square inch of the place already. And it had been days since the murder. Faith would have gotten rid of any evidence that pointed to her.

Would Sydney have to break into her house and search for clues like Glenda had originally suggested? It still sounded like a terrible idea, but Sydney didn't have any good ideas to try instead.

Her phone buzzed on the coffee table, and she lunged for it.

Javier
I didn't find out much. The police haven't officially charged Logan yet, but they suspect him of the murder.

Sydney
Why him of all people?

Javier
He owes a lot of money, apparently. Took out some big loans to start the restaurant.
And they know he was in the vicinity that night.

Sydney
He's there every night. The man's a workaholic.

Javier
Hey, I'm not the one accusing him.

Sydney
Sorry.
And thanks again. I appreciate you finding this out for me.

She practically fell onto the couch. They hadn't charged him, and the evidence they had sounded very circumstantial. No bloody crowbars found in the trunk of his car or security footage of him breaking into the bakery. That was good, right?

Javier
There's one more thing.

Sydney stared at the screen, dread worming its way into her stomach. A text message hadn't looked so ominous since the first time she'd been messaged by Glenda's ghost.

Javier
Apparently he has a criminal record.

Sydney
Logan?

Javier
Yeah.
I don't know exactly what, but it sounded serious.

Sydney barely paid attention to what she typed as she and Javier said goodbye. She stared ahead at the TV, not processing the images that flashed across the screen. A criminal record? That couldn't be right. Logan gave off a bit of a bad boy vibe, but not *that* much.

She should be able to find out. Those kinds of records were public, weren't they? She opened her laptop.

It took a long time, but she eventually found it: assault charges from over a decade earlier. Her stomach dropped.

Logan had said he spent his youth getting into trouble. Apparently he hadn't been kidding.

Chapter 12

Ice cream can't fix this

Sydney
Are you home?

Alex
Yeah. What's up?

Sydney
Logan got arrested.

Alex
OMG I knew he was sketchy.
That's so scary. Are you okay?

Sydney was not okay. She was slouched on the sofa, drinking her second glass of wine. She'd put the bottle on the coffee table so she wouldn't have to go to the kitchen to pour herself a refill. She hadn't had the energy to cook dinner, so she'd made instant ramen.

Her stomach was going to hate her tomorrow.

Sydney
It looks bad, but I still don't think he did it.
Part of me anyway.
Is that hopelessly naive?

Alex
It's not naive to want to see the best in people.
Completely normal actually.

Sydney
Normal can bite me.
I should just accept it. I finally meet a guy I like, so of course he turns out to be a murderer. That's life.

Alex
That's not life. There are good people out there.
Just not this guy.
Or the last girl I dated.
Though I guess cheating is pretty tame compared to murder.

Sydney
Ugh. Celina. I'd almost forgotten how much I hate her.
I need to add eggs to my grocery list so I can egg her house.

Alex
And I need to buy a baseball bat for this Logan guy.

Sydney
Violent much?

Alex
That's what sisters are for.
You eat some ice cream and take care of yourself until I can drop by and hug you, okay?

Sydney
Okay.

• • •

Sydney had the next day off thanks to trading shifts with Javier. With the bakery closed for two days after Glenda's murder, Sydney had barely worked at all lately. If the week had gone normally, she would be relishing the chance to kick up her feet and relax.

At the moment, she felt less excited and more lethargic. It was after one, and she hadn't changed out of her pajamas or done anything productive yet. Her stomach had roiled all morning in revenge for her drinking and terrible dinner the night before, and she'd tried to make amends by having a healthy soup for lunch. It hadn't helped, so she'd made herself a decadent dessert out of spite. She was partway through a marathon of *The Addams Family* when her phone dinged.

Marissa
I'm sorry about Caleb. I should've known he was off-limits.

Sydney wanted to ignore her. She returned her gaze to the TV for a few minutes before pausing it in resignation. The text had distracted her, and she wouldn't be able to focus until she replied.

Sydney
He's not off-limits.
I'm not mad you two hooked up. I just wish you would've told me first.

Marissa
I know I should have.
I just wanted to avoid the awkwardness.

Sydney
This is more awkward.

Marissa
Yeah…
Sorry.

Sydney debated whether to forgive her. She could nurse her grudge and give Marissa the cold shoulder whenever she saw her at the bakery—which would be a lot. Honestly that seemed like it would punish herself as much as it did Marissa. Besides, that would mean ending their friendship over *Caleb*, and he wasn't worth it.

Sydney
I'll get over it.
Not a big deal compared to everything else going on.

Marissa
Yeah, I'm sorry about that guy next door.
I know you liked him.

Sydney
I should've expected it.
Honestly, it's just my luck.

Marissa
That's a depressing outlook—even for you.
We need to cheer you up.

Sydney
I'm working on it.

She snapped a photo of the half-devoured brownie topped with ice cream sitting in a bowl on her coffee table.

Marissa
Nice.
I'll see you tomorrow then. Enjoy.

Sydney took another bite of ice cream and ignored the unhappy rumble from her stomach. She hit the Play button on her remote and shifted into a more comfortable position on the couch. Tired despite not having done anything all day, she tried to lose herself in *The Addams Family*. Gomez and Morticia were such a perfect couple. What dark forces did Sydney have to sell her soul to in order to get a happy relationship like that?

She remained on the couch all afternoon, only getting up to use the bathroom and refill her glass of water. *Go for a jog,* urged the responsible voice in the back of her head. *Vacuum the apartment. For the love of all things holy, at least put on a clean shirt.*

Sydney ignored it and started a new episode, but her phone buzzed a second later and she had to hit Pause again.

Glenda
Any news from the arrest?

Sydney stared. She hadn't expected to hear from Glenda again. Thinking back to their last conversation, she squirmed uncomfortably on top of the couch cushions.

Well, if Marissa could eat a slice of humble pie and apologize, then so could Sydney.

Sydney
Look, I'm sorry about what I said yesterday.
I was out of line.

Glenda
You were.
But it seems I've been out of line for a long time now
It's funny how I only realize it now that it's too late to change anything.

Sydney's thumbs hovered uncertainly over the screen. She had no idea how to deal with a contrite, self-aware Glenda. It was like encountering a cat that wanted to play Frisbee.

Sydney
What are you still doing here? I thought you would've moved on or whatever.

Glenda

I thought so too.

Now I'm thinking maybe Logan isn't the real culprit after all.

Honestly, what's the point of me being able to contact you from beyond the grave if the police were just going to catch the murderer anyway? They must have the wrong person.

Sydney

I don't know.

We can't make assumptions about why this whole ghost texting thing is happening.

And Logan has a criminal record. We know he was near the scene of the crime. He has a motive. It all makes sense.

Glenda

What happened? Yesterday you were swearing he was innocent.

Sydney looked away from the words as if that could lessen their sting. Yesterday felt like forever ago.

Sydney

Just because I like him doesn't mean he's innocent.

I need to face facts.

Glenda

You should trust your instincts.

Sydney

Yesterday you said your instincts told you he was a crook.

Glenda

Well, I was wrong.

I don't want to be stuck here forever, Sydney.

You don't owe me anything, but please. Keep investigating.

Sydney looked up at the ceiling, feeling like someone had just thrown a twenty-pound backpack over her shoulders.

Did she really want to do this again? Just look at her: she had a chocolate stain on her T-shirt, and she stank from lack of showering. Would investigating again make her feel better, or would it just make things worse?

Sydney
I don't know where to go from here.
But I'll think about it.

She thought about it—hard. She turned off the TV and stared at the blank screen for a while. She paced around the living room and then got out the vacuum cleaner, figuring she might as well do something productive if she was going to be walking around the apartment anyway.

She thought of Logan sitting in a jail cell, of the police surrounding the bakery on the morning Glenda's body was discovered. She remembered Faith's tearstained face.

Faith was the only person Sydney hadn't ruled out. She brought up her social media profiles and browsed through them. Faith didn't post very frequently and mostly uploaded family photos. The most recent ones showed her children doing winter activities like building snowmen in the front yard. One showed Faith and her wife at a restaurant with the caption DATE NIGHT, and another gushed proudly about their daughter winning second place at the school science fair. Sydney had to scroll all the way back to December to find a picture that included Glenda. She was sitting on a couch between her grandchildren, Christmas presents in her lamp and an uncharacteristic smile on her face.

It sent a wave of sadness through Sydney. All she'd ever seen of Glenda was her grouchy, unreasonable side at work, but the woman had a life outside the bakery: people she cared about and hobbies she enjoyed. The killer had taken that from her.

Scrolling through Faith's timeline, Sydney found nothing to indicate she had a difficult relationship with her mother.

No passive-aggressive comments or posts that referenced an argument. But that was social media: it presented an ideal life, not a real one.

Sydney would have to get off her butt and search something other than a computer if she wanted to find evidence Faith had murdered Glenda. Faith had been the last person to leave the bakery and see Glenda alive. She had a reason to want Glenda dead. Who else could have done it? Sydney had ruled out everyone else with a key.

Or had she? She knew Marissa, Faith, Javier, and Caleb all had keys, but were there more out there? Did the landlord have a spare in case of emergencies? And hadn't Caleb lost his once before?

Sydney didn't know how to check with the landlord, but confirming Caleb hadn't dropped his on the sidewalk or left it lying around his apartment for one of his sketchy friends to pick up should be easy enough.

Sydney
Hey. Do you still have your key to the bakery?

Caleb
Hey, sexy.
Yeah, why? Do you need it?

Sydney
I need you to be absolutely positive you still have it.
Are you sure you didn't drop it somewhere?

Caleb
I'm looking at it on my key chain right now.

Dang it. So much for that theory. Sydney would have to see about approaching the landlord. Maybe she could ask Faith? She could give the excuse that she was worried about the killer getting inside again. It would be a good chance to talk to Faith about the murder and see if she had an alibi.

Caleb
You want to come over tonight?

Oh right. She had to deal with Caleb first.

Sydney
Just me and you?

Caleb
That's right.

Sydney
No, thanks then.

Caleb
Why not? I thought we said we'd still be friends.

Sydney
Yeah, so I'll hang out with you in a group or out somewhere, but not alone in your apartment.

Sydney needed to keep herself away from temptation. Sure, the guy she currently liked might be locked up in jail, and yeah, he might actually be a killer who deserved it, but that didn't mean she wanted to start things up with her ex-boyfriend again.

Even if a night of no-strings-attached fun with him might help relieve some of her pent-up stress.

No. That was probably what Marissa had been thinking. Sydney had to stay strong and keep herself away from him.

Caleb
Come on. Can't we be friends with benefits?

Sydney
No.

I don't have time for this, Caleb.

Caleb
Help a guy out. I haven't gotten laid in weeks.

That lying son of a gun. See? This was why she needed to stay away from him. She couldn't trust him about anything.

Sydney
What about Marissa?

Caleb
What about her?
She's not going to be my booty call. She hates me.

Sydney
But you two hooked up on Saturday.
She told me.

A few seconds passed, and she pictured him desperately trying to come up with an excuse. Would he call Marissa a liar? Invent a twin brother? Claim he had amnesia?

Caleb
Oh yeah. Just the one time though.

Sydney frowned at the phone. Since when did Caleb admit he'd done something wrong? She'd like to think he'd matured as a person, but his response sent a signal of suspicion through her brain.

Sydney
You're not even going to try to deny it?

Caleb
No. I won't lie.

But he lied all the time. The second time they'd broken up, it was because he'd told her he was going to spend Saturday helping his friend move, and an hour later she'd found his friend posting photos of the two of them at a strip club.

Sydney hadn't been mad at him for going to a strip club at three in the afternoon. She would have tagged along if he'd invited her. It was the lying that had spurred her to dump him.

Though it hadn't been enough to stop her from hooking up with him again two weeks later. Sometimes Sydney wanted to smack herself.

Sydney
Then why did you say you haven't gotten laid in weeks?

Caleb
I forgot.

Sydney
You forgot?

Caleb
Yeah. I must have been drunk.

Sydney
But you remember now?

Caleb
Yeah. We definitely hooked up on Saturday. She came to my apartment right after work. It was a little after four. She stayed there overnight and left around seven the next morning.

You're not mad, are you?

Okay, that was a lot of specific, unasked-for detail. That signal of suspicion in her brain turned into a ringing alarm.

Sydney

Did she really come over, or are you making this up?

Caleb

It really happened.

If you don't want to hang out tonight, that's fine. I'll talk to you later.

Sydney

What aren't you telling me?

She waited for a response, but nothing came. The alarm turned into a wailing siren with flashing lights. He was definitely hiding something.

She shot to her feet and headed for her closet to change clothes. Sydney didn't know how to investigate a murder. She didn't know how her phone could receive text messages from the afterlife or why any of this was happening.

But if she knew one thing, it was how to get a straight answer out of Caleb Bray.

• • •

Caleb lived in a one-story gray apartment building. It was long and narrow with four units side by side. A few doors had decorations: welcome signs, floral wreaths, or potted plants by the walkway. Caleb's door was bare except for the dent he'd made when moving in his pool table. (He never used it except to pile laundry on top of.) A small pond lay next to the building, which had attracted a flock of geese. Sydney thought of Logan wistfully before knocking on the door.

Caleb opened it and smiled widely when he saw her.

"Hey, babe," he said. "I knew you'd change your mind."

Sydney stormed inside so he couldn't shut the door in her face, forcing him to scramble back a few steps. "What happened on Saturday? Tell me the truth."

He smiled nervously. "What? Babe, if you're jealous of me and Marissa—"

"I'm not jealous. I've dated you on and off for almost two years. I know when you're lying to me."

Beads of sweat formed on his forehead. "I'm not lying."

She jabbed her finger into his chest. "Bull crap. What really happened on Saturday?"

"Marissa came over—"

"Caleb, I swear, if you don't fess up in the next five seconds, I'll—"

"You'll what?" He lifted his chin and looked at her daringly. "Yell at me some more? Nag me constantly? Come on, Sydney. You can't force me to tell you anything."

Sydney went still. That was practically a confession that he was hiding something, but it wasn't enough. She needed him to say it straight out and in detail. She was so close to a breakthrough, but what if he was right? She couldn't tie him to a chair and smack him until he admitted the truth, and she'd blown her chance to sweet-talk him into revealing the information. What other options did she have?

If she couldn't get information out of *Caleb* of all people, then what hope did she have with anybody else?

She took a step back and peered at him. *Come on, Sydney. Think.* She knew Caleb, knew what he loved and what he hated. She'd dated him for so long; there must be some piece of information in her brain that could help her.

Then it hit her.

"If you don't fess up in the next five seconds, I'll become your crazy ex-girlfriend," she said.

He just stared, uncomprehending.

"You think this is bad?" she asked. "Imagine me banging on your bedroom window and screaming whenever you bring a girl over. I'll visit every bar you like and tell everyone that you can only last sixty seconds in bed and your equipment is small. We hang out with the same people. They'll read every word when I post embarrassing stories about you online. I can make your life miserable, Caleb, so *talk*."

He threw his hands into the air. "All right, all right! Marissa didn't really come over."

Sydney realized she'd practically backed him into a wall. She took a step backward to give him room to breathe.

"Then why did you lie?" she asked.

"It was her idea. You know we both thought Glenda was a grumpy old bag. With her dead, the police would be looking at her enemies, and neither of us had an alibi. We made up the story to keep ourselves safe."

Sydney felt dizzy. If neither of them had alibis, then…

Then she knew who killed Glenda.

"So I didn't really sleep with Marissa," Caleb said. "You've got no reason to be mad. We can still… you know."

He smoothed back his hair. Sydney blinked at him, so wrapped up in her own thoughts that she didn't understand him at first.

"What part of 'we're done' didn't you understand?" she asked. "I'll see you later, Caleb."

And she walked off, pulling out her phone to text Glenda.

Chapter 13

Cake and other dangers

The next morning, Sydney pulled into the parking lot in front of the bakery and stared. The building had no business looking so ominous, especially not with a pink sign bearing the image of a cupcake and smiling sun. She'd only managed to get down a piece of toast for breakfast and felt it slosh around queasily in her stomach.

Her phone chimed.

Glenda
I don't know about this, Sydney. It seems dangerous.

Sydney
I don't have a choice.
The cops didn't believe me. I need to prove it somehow.

Glenda
But if Marissa realizes what you're doing, she might kill you to cover her tracks.

As if Sydney hadn't considered that possibility. She turned up the volume on the rock song playing over the car speakers, hoping to pump herself up as she typed her reply.

Sydney
But if I don't do this, you could be stuck in limbo forever, and Logan could spend years in jail for a crime he didn't commit.
I have to try.

Glenda
Just be careful.

Sydney
I will.
Believe me, I don't want to die and get stuck with you for all eternity.
Can you imagine? I'd say we'd murder each other, but we couldn't even do that.

Glenda
Not funny.

Sydney
It's a little funny.

Glenda
Text me when you're done, okay?

Sydney
Will do. Wish me luck.

Glenda
Good luck.

• • •

8:30
Glenda
Just checking in. How is the plan going?

8:39
Glenda
Is everything okay?

8:45
Glenda
Sydney, please let me know you're all right.

8:53
Glenda
Sydney???

• • •

At 6:55, Sydney walked into the bakery and took a deep breath. Faith was already in the office and said good morning as Sydney clocked in. The enormous, upside-down chandelier cake had been assembled during her day off and hung suspended from a gleaming silver stand. It still needed fondant and the final decorations before they delivered it that afternoon.

The bell over the shop door rang as Marissa walked in, and every muscle in Sydney's body tensed.

"Hey," Marissa said with a smile. "Feeling better?"

"Yeah," Sydney lied.

They got to work, and Sydney wondered…

What if she was wrong? What if Marissa wasn't the killer? Would she ever forgive Sydney for accusing her? Would Sydney ever forgive herself?

Customers came in and out as the morning passed, and with Faith in her office, Sydney couldn't enact her plan. It was a quarter past eight by the time Faith left to make some morning deliveries. A middle-aged man searched the display case for a good ten minutes before selecting the perfect macaroons for an anniversary present. When he left, the bakery was empty except for Marissa and Sydney.

They worked in the kitchen, keeping the door open so they could hear if another customer came inside. Sydney's stomach twisted into knots, and her hands shook as she poured batter into a baking pan, spilling a quarter of it onto the table. She set down the bowl and tried to calm herself.

She couldn't back down. People were counting on her. She hadn't asked for this job solving murders for the dead, but she'd gotten it all the same. If she didn't catch the murderer, no one would.

She reached for her phone in her pocket and turned on the audio recorder she'd prepared. Then she checked that the pepper spray canister was still in her other pocket.

She took another deep breath. She didn't want to do this. She *really* didn't want to do this.

But she had to.

Rehearsing her speech in her mind, she turned around to confront Marissa…

…and found the woman standing behind her with a knife.

"Caleb told me he snitched to you," Marissa said. "You shouldn't have depended on him to keep a secret."

Her eyes looked like they belonged to another person; they were so cold and hard.

Sydney froze, and it took her a second to find her voice. "I could say the same to you."

"You don't seem surprised. I knew you'd figure it out."

She waved the knife wildly, making Sydney press herself against the table in an attempt to back away.

"Why did you have to go poking around?" Marissa demanded. "Couldn't you just let it be? It's Glenda, for crying out loud. Who cares that she's dead? We're all better off."

"Faith would disagree. So would Logan, considering he's stuck in jail right now for a crime *you* committed."

"So that's what this is about? A guy?" Marissa's eyes bulged. Strands of her hair stuck to her sweaty forehead, and her voice took on a shrieking edge. "I've been your friend for years, Sydney. You should be on my side, not his."

"You killed a person, Marissa." Sydney hated how soft and weak her voice sounded. "I don't think you came in here planning to, but you still did."

"You don't know anything."

"I—" Sydney stared at the knife and swallowed. "I think you clocked out on Saturday night without asking Glenda for a raise. You trudged to your car, resigned to going home in defeat, but then you changed your mind."

Sydney's voice gained volume the more she spoke, and she stood straighter. "You gathered your courage and marched back inside to ask her. And when you saw her alone, the safe open with all that money…" She glanced toward the office where it had happened. "You struck. Probably with the missing rolling pin, though I'm not sure about that part." She looked back at Marissa. "And you got blood on your jacket, didn't you? That's why you were wearing a new one the next day."

Marissa's eyes went distant, and Sydney thought about the pepper spray in her pocket. Her hand twitched, but she was too afraid to move.

"She deserved it." Marissa's voice came out hoarse. "She treated us like dirt. She paid us crap. I was just taking what she owed me."

"You took her life," Sydney said. "She didn't owe that to—"

Marissa lunged at her with the knife.

Sydney screamed and jumped aside. Scared out of her frozen stupor, she yanked the pepper spray out of her pocket and aimed it at Marissa's face.

Marissa slashed at her. Burning pain erupted in Sydney's hand, and she dropped the canister. It hit the tile floor with a metallic clang and rolled away.

"I shouldn't have to do this!" Marissa shouted. "You should have understood!"

Sydney scrambled back, clutching her bleeding hand to her chest. Did she still have all her fingers? How deep was the cut? She couldn't afford to look closely at it. Marissa stalked toward her, and there was nowhere to go. The door was on the opposite side of the room. Sydney looked frantically toward it, hoping for a customer, a coworker—anyone.

"You can't murder me in broad daylight," Sydney said breathlessly. "The cops will find you. Logan can't take the fall for this one."

"But Caleb can." Marissa eyed her as if assessing the best place to stab. "Especially when I plant the knife in his apartment."

Sydney jerked her head back and forth. "It won't work. You're right here. You'll be the prime suspect. The only reason you got away with killing Glenda is luck. You think you can cover up a second murder? No one's that lucky."

"I have to try. What other choice do I have?"

Marissa stalked toward her, and Sydney backed away. Hot blood dripped down her hand and splattered onto the tile floor. What should she do? Maybe if she could get to the shelves, she could grab a knife and use it to defend herself. But the only things near her were the spice rack and that giant wedding cake.

The cake.

Sydney turned slightly, backing toward it.

"How about you choose not to commit a second homicide?" she asked. "Come on, Marissa. Look at yourself. Is this who you want to be?"

The knife shook in Marissa's hand. "No, but it's what I have to do."

She lunged.

Sydney dove to the left.

Marissa stumbled, and as she pivoted, Sydney grabbed the massive cake, heaved, and…

Over one hundred pounds of cake, cream, and fondant crashed on top of Marissa.

Sydney stood there, breathing heavily as her former friend groaned from the floor. Crumbled cake, splattered buttercream, and torn fondant covered both her and surrounding tile. Eyes closed, Marissa didn't move. Had she hit her head when she'd fallen? Sydney certainly hoped so.

She raced outside. Then, with her nonbleeding hand, she pulled out her phone and called the police.

Chapter 14

It's over (finally)

Later that morning, Sydney sat at one of the tables in front of the bakery as police cars and ambulances once again filled the parking lot. The paramedics had already seen her and bandaged up her right hand. She'd been lucky. Not only had she kept all her fingers, but the cut was shallow enough that she wouldn't need stitches.

She took a bite of the double-chocolate cupcake she'd snagged from the display case before getting kicked out of the building. Nobody could argue she hadn't earned it.

She stared around the strip mall. A few onlookers crowded the sidewalk, held back by yellow crime scene tape. Some drivers slowed down so they could peer out their car windows at the scene. There was even a limo in the parking lot, sleek, black, and completely out of place. There wasn't a high school prom or anything else happening today, and she couldn't imagine any other reason someone would rent a limo to drive around Beaverfield of all places. Its windows were tinted, so she couldn't see inside as it sidled slowly by.

Weird.

Tired of being stared at, she pulled out her phone.

Sydney
Hey, sorry for the late reply.

Glenda
Thank goodness.
Are you okay?

Sydney
I've got a nasty cut on my hand where Marissa tried to slice me apart, but otherwise yeah.

Glenda
We're lucky it wasn't worse.
So it really was Marissa, then.

Sydney
Yeah. When the cops showed up, she tried to tell them I attacked her.
But I had the whole thing recorded, so that didn't work out so well.

Glenda
The nerve of her.
Hopefully her jail sentence will give her time to reflect and accept responsibility for her crimes.

Sydney
Yeah, somehow I doubt that.

Glenda
Well, I'm glad you're alive and even gladder you texted.
I wasn't sure how much longer I could hold out.

Sydney sat up straighter.

Sydney
What do you mean?

Glenda
It's time for me to move on. I can feel it.

Sydney
Oh.
I don't know what to say.

She truly didn't. The fact that Glenda was dead… It hadn't really sunk in with Sydney texting her every day. But if Glenda was moving on, then this was the end. She would go off to discover what waited beyond death, and Sydney wouldn't join her for what she hoped would be a very long time.

Glenda
You don't have to say anything.
I'm the one who needs to say thank you.
If you hadn't helped, I'd probably be trapped here forever, and the person who murdered me would be working in the same building as my daughter.
I know I haven't always treated you the best, and I appreciate what you did for me.

Sydney
Glad I could help.
Honestly I'm just relieved I figured out it was Marissa.

Glenda
Can I ask you one more favor?

Sydney
Sure.

Glenda
Could you look out for Faith and the bakery?

Sydney glanced over to where Faith was pacing up and down the sidewalk as she spoke to someone on the phone. She'd come back from her deliveries a few minutes after the police had shown up, and Sydney had explained what had happened.

It was the first time she'd ever heard the sweet, soft-spoken woman swear.

Sydney
Yeah. I'd do that anyway.

Glenda
Thank you, Sydney.
And goodbye.

Sydney
Goodbye, Glenda.

Sydney lowered her phone, and if anyone noticed the tears in her eyes, hopefully they'd put it down to trauma from the attack.

• • •

The police eventually let Sydney go home, warning that they might need to call her into the station later for more questioning. She sent a text to Logan.

Sydney
Hey. Text me how you're doing when you get a chance.

He didn't respond, and she wondered if they'd released him yet. Bringing her phone into the bathroom so she'd hear the chime when he replied, she started a hot bath and tossed in one of her new bath bombs.

She'd just sunk into it and started to let her body relax when her phone buzzed. But it wasn't Logan.

Alex
Let me get this straight.
Marissa is a murderer.
You confronted her—alone.
Without telling anyone what you were doing.
With only pepper spray for backup.

And no other plan for what to do if she attacked?

Sydney
Of course it sounds bad when you put it like that.

Alex
If you EVER do something like this again, you are dead.
Because I'll murder you.
Just so we're clear.

Sydney
We're clear.

Alex
Good.
Dinner tomorrow night? I need some sibling bonding time.

Sydney
Sounds good.

She finished the rest of the bath with no interruptions, a soothing vanilla scent clinging to her skin even after she got out. She was partway through making a grilled cheese sandwich for a late lunch when her phone buzzed again. Her heart leaped, hoping for a response from Logan, but again she was disappointed.

Faith
How are you feeling? Do you need to take tomorrow off?

Sydney
I'd rather come in.
Keeping busy seems like a good idea right now.
Though I might need some help since my hand's all bandaged up.

Faith
I already asked Kendall and Javier if they could come in.

Sydney

I'm guessing the schedule's a mess with Marissa gone.

Faith

I still can't believe she did it.

And yes, the schedule's a wreck. No amount of color-coded highlighting can fix it.

I'm stressing out—and that bridezilla must have yelled at me for ten straight minutes about not getting her cake, which didn't help.

Sydney

Attempted murder wasn't a good enough excuse for her??

Faith

Apparently not.

I'm expecting the awful review to show up online any day now.

Good grief. This was why so many people in the wedding catering business burned out and closed shop. The customers were ridiculous.

Faith

I don't know what to do. The bakery was so important to Mom, and I can't imagine working anywhere else.

But we're short-staffed and behind schedule. It's going to take time to train someone new.

The next month or so is going to be rough.

Sydney

Are you looking to vent, or do you want advice?

Faith

I'm open to advice.

Sydney

Offer Javier a full-time position. He's been wanting to upgrade.

Faith

And he wouldn't need any training! He knows the business inside and out.

Sydney, you're brilliant.

Sydney

I have my moments.

Faith

I need to run some numbers and talk to Javier. I'll see you tomorrow.

Sydney went back to cooking lunch, buoyed by a sense of satisfaction. She still needed to apologize to Javier in person for basically accusing him of murder, but at least her meddling might help him land a full-time job.

She spent the rest of the day lounging, though it felt a lot different than the lethargic funk she'd been in the day earlier. She was wearing clean clothes for one thing, and she'd opened all the blinds to let in sunlight so she didn't feel trapped in a dark cave. She felt exhausted but in a good way, like she'd finished a hard workout and was taking some well-earned rest.

Or at least she imagined that's what it would feel like if she actually worked out.

She texted her dad to let him know what happened before he heard it from someone else (like Alex). He pretended he'd known Marissa was a bad apple ever since she and Sydney used to hang out in high school. Sydney had rolled her eyes and gone along with it, making plans to visit him on her next day off. Then she settled on the couch with a good book.

It was late afternoon when she finally got her long-awaited reply from Logan.

Logan
Hey.
I'm all right.
Happy to be home. Annoyed I'm behind schedule. Depressed this whole thing happened in the first place.

Sydney
I feel that.

Logan
How are you doing?
I heard the murderer was another of the employees at the bakery?

Sydney
Marissa, yeah.
She has problems.

Logan
Were you friends?

Sydney felt a hollow ache in her chest. She hadn't taken time yet to mourn the loss of Marissa's friendship. She guessed it would hit her later.

Sydney
Emphasis on the past tense.

Logan
Sorry.

Sydney
It's fine.
I just wished I'd realized it was her before yesterday. I could've saved you a lot of grief.

Logan
Wait. Yesterday?

Sydney
Yeah. I tried telling the police, but they didn't believe me. It figures I'd have to get attacked by a knife-wielding murderer to get taken seriously.

His reply didn't come for several seconds.

Logan
I'm sorry. What exactly happened while I was locked up?

Sydney
They didn't tell you when they released you?

Logan
Just that someone from the bakery got brought in.
You got attacked? Are you all right?

Sydney
Just a small cut. I'm fine.
I tried to be clever and trick her into confessing, and it didn't quite work out the way I'd planned.

Logan
So you were what—investigating her?

Sydney shifted atop the couch, debating how much to tell him. Was there any way she could avoid the fact that, for a while, she'd thought he was guilty? But she didn't want to pull a Caleb and lie to him. If the spark she felt between them was going to grow into anything, she needed to be open and honest from the start.

Except for the whole texting dead people thing. There was just no good way to bring that up.

Sydney
Not at first.

I thought it was one of my other coworkers for a while.
Or you.

Logan
I give off murderer vibes, huh?

Sydney
The opposite actually. I thought you were too good to be true. Then I found out about your criminal record, and I was just in a bad, suspicious headspace.

Logan
Oh.

Great. Suspicion and nosiness probably weren't qualities he was looking for in a potential partner. Sydney wanted to throw another cake at Marissa for getting her into this situation. After they charged her with murder, they should charge her with sabotaging Sydney's first budding relationship with a decent guy in years.

Sydney
That was a creepy invasion of your privacy, huh?
You'll have to cut me some slack. My boss was murdered in the building where I work, and I was paranoid.

Logan
It ended with you clearing my name, so I guess I should be thanking you.
And I'll understand if you don't want to see me again.

Sydney nearly dropped her phone. Her fingers moved so fast that she kept mistyping her reply. She hurriedly deleted the typos and tried again.

Sydney
What? Why wouldn't I want to see you?

I figured you'd be the one mad at me.

Three little dots appeared as he typed his response, but then they vanished, and no text came. What had he been trying to say?

Sydney
Wait, is this because of the whole criminal record thing? That was a decade ago. It's not going to scare me off. You're not doing crimes now, are you?

Logan
No.
Even if I hadn't grown as a person, I've worked too hard and am too close to success to risk it.

Sydney
Then we're good.

Logan
All right then.
I'd still like to know what you've been up to while I was locked up.

Sydney
It's kind of a long story.

Logan
Tell it to me over lunch tomorrow?

She leaned back, her mouth curving into a smile.

Sydney
Deal.

Note from the Author

Thank you for reading! Do you want to find out how Sydney and Logan's lunch date went? Visit KristenBrand.com/Newsletter to join my mailing list, and as a thank-you gift, you'll get a copy of *The Second Date*, a short story set the day after the events of this book. There may be kissing. Or there may not. You'll have to read to find out. ;)

Dead Messages is my first foray into the cozy mystery genre, and I hope you enjoyed it. Thanks again for your support!

Poison Contact

Texts From Beyond, Book 2

Not ready to say goodbye to Beaverfield and all its quirky (and occasionally murderous) inhabitants? Check out *Dead Messages'* sequel, *Poison Contact*:

It starts with an order of inappropriately shaped cookies for a bachelorette party.

When Sydney Farina, professional baker and amateur sleuth, delivers the cookies, the bride-to-be drops dead right in front of her. Sydney tries to convince herself the mysterious tragedy is none of her business, but the rude bride who texted her for constant updates about her order doesn't stop texting now that she's dead. And her ghost begs Sydney to solve her murder and clear her fiancé's name.

Sydney isn't sure the fiancé is innocent, but it's hard to ignore the desperate ghost. As she investigates the bride's frenemies and former lovers, she finds few leads and starts to worry she'll never put the bride's ghost to rest.

But she must be getting close to the truth, because the killer is trying to silence her… permanently.

Twice the length of Dead Messages, Poison Contact has more mystery, more murder attempts, and more texts from beyond the grave. Order now and start the investigation!

ABOUT THE AUTHOR

If Kristen Brand could have any superpower, she'd want telekinesis so she wouldn't have to move from her computer to pour a new cup of tea. She lives in Florida with her husband, and her hobbies include reading comic books and desperately trying to keep the plants in her garden alive. An author of fantasy, superhero fiction, and now cozy mystery, she writes stories with fire-forged friends, explosive fight scenes, and kissing. Learn more about her books at KristenBrand.com.

www.ingramcontent.com/pod-product-compliance
Ingram Content Group UK Ltd.
Pitfield, Milton Keynes, MK11 3LW, UK
UKHW041956190726
13854UKWH00005B/2013

9 798201 289119